PURRFECT KILL

THE MYSTERIES OF MAX 17

NIC SAINT

PURRFECT KILL

The Mysteries of Max 17

Copyright © 2020 by Nic Saint

Edited by Chereese Graves

www.nicsaint.com

Give feedback on the book at: info@nicsaint.com

facebook.com/nicsaintauthor
@nicsaintauthor

First Edition

Printed in the U.S.A

*C*hickie Hay was shaking her athletic frame to the beat, one eye on the floor-to-ceiling mirror, the other on the big screen where her choreo was being demonstrated by her personal choreographer Tracy Marbella. Chickie's next tour was coming up and she needed to get in shape, which is why she was working up a sweat practicing her moves and rehearsing the concert playlist until she had the songs and the dance routines down pat.

"Baby, baby," she sang, the music thumping through the room. She was wearing her usual pink leggings and her favorite pink sweatshirt—the same outfit she always wore when she started rehearsals. They were worn out by now, after years of use, but Chickie had a superstitious streak, and wouldn't wear anything except her lucky threads.

"Baby, baby, baby," she sang as she swung her hips and thrust out her arms.

She'd have preferred it if her trusty choreographer had been with her in person, to make those small corrections and improvements that make all the difference, but Tracy hadn't been able to make it. Doctor's appointment. No worries, though. Tracy always filmed her choreos and gave her clients plenty to work with.

"Baby, baby, baby, baby…"

Chickie frowned at her image in the mirror. Something wasn't right and she couldn't put her finger on it. Tracy would know. The experienced choreographer would only need a glimpse to know what was wrong and immediately correct her. 'No, Chickie—you need to relax those shoulders. And be light on your feet. Lighter! You look like an elephant stomping across the stage. Snappy movements. Snappy, snappy, snappy!'

And Chickie, even though she sometimes had a hard time following instructions, would do as she was told, because that's how much faith she put in Tracy's genius.

The fact of the matter was that she had a lot riding on the new album and the accompanying tour. It was her first one in five years, and already the media were calling it her comeback album. Then again, if you didn't put out something new every six months, you were already a has-been and ripe for a much-touted comeback.

She was proud of the new album. And felt that it was probably the best thing she'd ever done. She just hoped her fans, her Chickies, would like the new stuff. She'd invited a select few of them to the house the week before for a slumber party, so they could hear the new songs, and they'd loved them. Loved them! One or two had even fainted. Fainting was good. It was a sign she still had what it took to inspire her army of Chickies.

The sound of a pebble hitting the window had her look up in surprise. She walked over and looked out. It took another pebble to direct her attention to a tree whose branches reached the fence. One of her most fanatical Chickies sat in the tree and was throwing rocks at her window. Oh, God. Not that guy again. But instead of indicating her displeasure, she gave him a little pinky wave. You had to keep the superfans happy.

She quickly moved back from the window before this self-declared #SuperChickie heaved a brick through the window and hit her smack in the face. Picking up her phone, she dialed Tyson's number, the man in charge of her small security crew.

"Yeah, Tyson. Olaf is back. He's sitting in a tree throwing rocks at my window. Can you get him out of there? Be nice about it—he may be nuts but he's still a fan. Thanks."

She shook her head in dismay. It was one thing to have fans but another to have crazies who followed you around wherever you went, trying to get a glimpse of you.

Trying to put the incident out of her mind, she resumed her rehearsal. One-step, two-step, pivot. One-step, two-step, pivot. Ouch. A sudden pain shot through her ankle.

"Oh, hell!" she cried, and threw up her hands. "Now see what you did, Olaf!"

And just as she picked up the phone to set up an appointment with her physiotherapist, the door swung open and she glanced up at the new arrival.

"Oh, hey," she said. "I think I twisted my ankle again. And it's all because of that horrible Olaf Poley. Can you believe he's actually throwing rocks at my window now?"

Suddenly two hands closed around her neck with surprising strength. She tried to fight back but to no avail. And as she started to lose consciousness, she remembered Tracy's words from their very first session: 'You need to work on your upper-body strength, missy! Train those noodles you call muscles until they're strong as iron bands!'

Oh, how she wished now she'd followed Tracy's advice.

I woke up from a strange sound. *Thump, thump, thump.* I could feel it in the pit of my stomach. As if some giant hand had grabbed the house and was shaking it all about.

And then I realized what it was.

"Earthquake!" I shouted as loud as I could. "Earthquake!"

And I was up and moving with great alacrity in the direction of the exit. I halted when a small inner voice told me I'd forgotten something. Something critical. I'd totally neglected to make sure my human was awake and responding to my cry of alarm.

So ignoring danger to life and limb, I turned back and checked on Odelia. Imagine my surprise when I saw that only Chase still occupied the bed, the covers pulled all the way up to his ears, blissfully sleeping the sleep of the dead in spite of my urgent plea.

"Earthquake!" I tooted in his ears. "Wake up, Chase—there's an earthquake!"

And to add credence to my words, I placed my paws on

the burly copper and started massaging his mighty chest, not stinting on the odd claw extending from the odd paw.

"Not now, Max," Chase muttered, then turned to his other side and kept on sleeping.

"But Chase! You have to wake up! There's an earthquake and if you don't get up right now the house will fall on top of our heads!"

"That's nice," Chase muttered, even though I'm sure he couldn't possibly have understood what I'd just said. Chase is one of those humans who can't comprehend cats. Well, I guess most humans fall into that category. Only Odelia, Chase's girlfriend and my very own personal human, can speak to me, as well as her mother and grandmother.

My gaze briefly raked the spot where Odelia should have been, and I reached out a tentative paw to touch the sheet. Still warm, so she must have gotten up just now. So why hadn't she alerted her boyfriend of the impending doom? Or me, for that matter?

And then, as I glanced around some more, I saw that there was one other individual missing from the picture: my best friend Dooley. I wasn't worried about him, though, as Dooley has the luxury of calling two homes his home, both Odelia's and her mom's, and had presumably opted to keep his own human next door company this particular night.

I decided to go in search of Odelia, as she seemed to be the only one who'd be able to rouse Chase from the land of slumber and into full wakefulness.

The loud noise that I'd identified as an earthquake had changed in pitch, and as I hurried out of the bedroom and into the corridor, suddenly I realized my mistake. It wasn't an earthquake but... music. Loud, thumping music. The kind that humans like to dance to.

Quickly putting two and two together I deduced that Odelia had gotten up early and was using these quiet moments before the dawn to perform some of that aerobics, as she calls it. She dresses up in fluorescent lycra and jumps around in sync with the music, watching other women donning similar attire do the same on her big TV screen.

So I waddled down the stairs, and the moment I arrived in the living room I discovered I'd been right on the money: there, jumping up and down and swinging her arms, was Odelia, dressed in pink, moving along to the beat of some very peculiar music.

And next to her sat Dooley, bobbing his head as if in approval of these proceedings.

I sidled up to him, after giving Odelia a once-over to determine if she was still of sound mind and body or had been bitten by some exotic bug and gone off her rocker. With humans you never know. They act sane and sensible one minute, and nuts the next.

"Have you been up long?" I asked as I hopped onto the couch and joined my friend.

"I woke up when Odelia got out of bed," said Dooley, who, judging from the way he was still bobbing his head to the beat, seemed to enjoy the extravaganza.

"I thought it was an earthquake," I intimated. "Until I realized it was Odelia."

"She's getting good at this aerobics thing, isn't she?" said Dooley proudly. "She's almost as good as those very lively ladies on TV."

Those lively ladies were kicking their legs so high into the air I winced, afraid something might give and they'd lose a limb or two.

"Yeah, she's improving with leaps and bounds," I agreed, though I still wasn't entirely sure whether the aerobics thing was good for her or detrimental to her health. "Why does she do it, though? I mean, what's the point of all this jumping and sweating?"

"She wants to get in shape," said Dooley, regurgitating the party line. Odelia had been talking about getting 'in' shape for weeks now, even though as far as I could tell she'd never been 'out' of shape. Odelia is a slim-limbed young woman with long blond hair and not an ounce of fat on her entire body. So why she would feel the need to put herself through this ordeal is frankly beyond me. But then I've never claimed to be the world's biggest expert on humans, and the peculiar species keeps confounding me every day.

"Next she'll want to run a marathon," I said.

"A marathon?" asked Dooley, as he smiled at the complicated movements Odelia was performing with gusto. "What's a marathon, Max?"

"It's where humans run for a really long time, like hours and hours and hours, and then at the end, when they're almost dead, the first three people get a medal."

"They run…"

"And run and run and then they run some more."

"So what are they chasing?"

"Like I said, these medals."

"Are they edible medals?"

"I don't think so."

"Are they worth a great deal of money?"

"Well, yes, I guess. There's usually a gold medal, a silver one and a bronze one."

"Then that must be the reason. They run so they can get a medal and then sell it and use the money to buy food. Humans don't do these things without a good reason."

"Yeah, I guess they don't."

"Running just for the heck of it would be crazy."

"It sure would."

"Irrational."

We watched Odelia jump up and down some more, the music making the walls quake.

"So do you think Odelia gets a medal if she gets the routine just right?" asked Dooley.

"I doubt it. There's no medals in aerobics."

"Then why does she do it?"

"Um…"

We shared a look of apprehension. It had suddenly dawned on us that our human might be going crazy. Jumping up and down for no good reason at all. Odelia paused, and now clapped her hands, just like the women in the video. She turned to us, panting and wiping sweat from her brow with a towel. "What are you guys talking about?" she asked.

"I was wondering if you'll get a medal if you get your routine just right," said Dooley.

Odelia laughed. "Oh, Dooley. No, I won't get a medal. But I'll feel really good when those endorphins start flooding my brain, and that's all the encouragement I need."

"She's doing it for the endorphins," said Dooley, sounding relieved that our human wasn't crazy. Then he turned to me. "What's an endorphin, Max? Is it like a dolphin?"

"I think so," I said. Though why Odelia needed dolphins in her brain I didn't know.

"Endorphins are hormones," said Odelia, now bending over and touching the floor with her hands. "When they flood your brain they make you feel happy. That's why they call them happy hormones. Plus, getting in shape makes my body happy and healthy. And you know what they say. *Mens sana in corpore sano.* Healthy body, healthy mind."

"Uh-huh," I said dubiously. "I thought it was an earthquake. So my body wasn't happy, and neither was my mind."

"I'm sorry, Max," she said. "But if I don't do this first thing in the morning I never get round to it. Is Chase up yet?"

"Almost. He was talking, but refused to get up when I told them about the earthquake."

"Best to let him sleep. He got home pretty late last night."

Chase had gone up to New York the night before, for a reunion with his ex-colleagues from the NYPD, the police force he'd worked for before moving to Hampton Cove.

"Chase should try napping," said Dooley. "It's very effective. Uncle Alec could put beds in the office so his officers can nap whenever they feel tired. Cats do it all the time."

"Great idea, Dooley," I said. "I love napping."

"And I'll bet it's great for those dolphins, too."

"I don't think my uncle will like the idea," said Odelia with a laugh. "But I'll tell him."

"Napping," said Dooley, "is the secret why cats are so vigorous, vivacious and vital."

On TV the routine had started up again, and moments later Odelia was jumping around again, the earthquake moving up on the Richter scale. To such an extent that moments later Chase came stomping down the stairs, rubbing his eyes and yawning widely. He stood watching Odelia while she tried to kick and touch the ceiling, then shook his head and moved into the kitchen to start up his precious coffeemaker.

Soon the sounds of Odelia's aerobics routine mingled nicely with Chase's baritone voice singing along. And as he rubbed his stubbled jaw and then stretched, a third person entered the fray: it was Marge, Odelia's mom, and she looked a little frazzled.

Odelia pressed pause on the remote, and stood, hands on knees, panting freely.

"Odelia, honey, I need your help," said Marge as she took a seat on the couch.

"Sure, anything," said Odelia, grabbing for her towel again.

"It's your grandmother."

Odelia closed her eyes and groaned. "What has she gone and done now?"

"You know how she agreed to sing backing vocals in your father's band? Well, she's just announced she's tired of playing second fiddle and she's starting a solo career."

"Of course she has," said Odelia as she toweled off and sat down next to her mother.

"She wants to be the next Beyoncé," said Marge.

"Beyoncé?" said Odelia with a laugh. "But... Gran can't even sing."

"Not to mention she's old enough to be Beyoncé's grandmother."

"Who's Beyoncé?" asked Dooley.

"A famous singer," I said. "And a very popular one, too."

"She's been nagging me to get her a singing coach," said Marge, "and just now she told me she wants me to find her a manager—one of those power managers that can launch her career straight into the stratosphere, on account of the fact that she doesn't have time to build it up slowly."

"And what did you tell her?"

Marge threw up her arms. "That I don't know the first thing about showbiz or power managers or singing coaches! And that if she wants to be the next Beyoncé maybe she should start by joining a singing competition. They'll be sure to tell her if she's any good."

"Good advice," said Chase, who was sipping from a cup of coffee and looking a little bleary-eyed. "The best way to knock some sense into your grandmother is to subject her to a nice round of criticism—just as long as it's not us who provide the criticism I'm sure she'll take it on the chin and move on to her next foolish whim."

"I sincerely hope that's all this is," said Marge. "With a husband in showbiz, and now an elderly parent, life is starting to get a little too showbizzy to my liking. Not only is Tex expecting me to go to every single one of his performances and cheer him on, soon Mom will expect me to go to all of her performances, too. And here I thought things slowed down once the kids were out of the house. Looks like things are just getting started!"

"Well, trust me, Mom," said Odelia as she patted her mother's arm. "I don't have any plans to go into show business, so there's that. And I'm sure Gran's ambitions will be as short-lived as most of her endeavors. I give it a month —tops."

"Speak of the devil," Chase muttered through half-closed lips.

Gran had just walked in, looking as sprightly and vivacious as ever. "Odelia!" she cried as she made a beeline for her granddaughter. "You're up. Good. Look, I need you to be honest with me. Do you think I've got what it takes to be the next Beyoncé?"

"Um... I don't know, Gran," said Odelia, treading carefully.

'Maybe you can sing something for us?" Chase suggested. "How about *Single Ladies?*"

Gran eyed Chase strangely. "Single ladies? You don't have to rub it in, young man. It's true I'm a single lady right now but it's not very nice of you to point that out. Very rude."

"No, that's the name of the song," said Chase. "*Single Ladies.*"

"Never heard of it," said Gran, still giving Chase a nasty look.

"Okay. So how about *Crazy in Love?*"

"I'm not, but thanks for the suggestion. I'll sing Beyoncé's biggest hit, shall I?" She took a deep breath, then placed her hands on her chest and closed her eyes. "*Some boys kiss me, some boys hug me, I think they're oka-ay,*" she bleated in a croaky voice.

"Gran?" said Odelia, interrupting the songbird. "That's Madonna, not Beyoncé."

"Shut up and let me sing. *Cause we're li-ving in a mate-rial world...*"

It sounded a little awful, I thought, and judging from the frozen looks on the faces of all those present I wasn't alone in my assessment. Finally, Gran finished the song and opened her arms in anticipation of the roaring applause she clearly felt she deserved. When the applause didn't come, she eyed us with annoyance.

"Well? What do you think?" she snapped.

"Um… not bad," said Odelia. "Not bad at all. But you know that's not Beyoncé, right?"

"'Of course it's Beyoncé. One of the woman's greatest hits. So how about you, Marge? What do you reckon? Knocked it out of the park, huh? Hit a home run?"

"Um…." said Marge, darting anxious glances at her daughter.

"Blown away," said Gran with a nod of satisfaction. "That's what I was going for. Chase?"

"Loved it," Chase lied smoothly. "Best Beyoncé imitation I've ever heard."

"Perhaps you should put a little more pep in your show, though," said Marge.

"Oh, you'll get all the pep you need. I've asked Beyoncé's choreographer to work with me and he graciously accepted. In fact we're starting rehearsals today."

"Beyoncé's choreographer is going to work with you?" asked Odelia.

"Sure. You all know him. My ex-boyfriend Dick Bernstein. He's worked with Beyoncé for years. Choreographed all of her big shows, here and overseas. I asked him and he immediately said yes. It's gonna be a smash, you guys. And now if you'll excuse me—I gotta get ready before Dick arrives. Oh, and Marge? Can you tell Tex I'm not coming in today? My career takes precedence over that silly receptionist business. Toodle-oo!"

And with these words she was off, leaving us all stunned.

Except for Dooley, who was still wondering, "So who's Beyoncé?"

---

2

*O*delia was just about to walk into her office, after dutifully informing her father that Gran wouldn't be coming in today because she needed to launch her career, when a loud honking sound waylaid her. She looked up and saw that her uncle was trying to catch her attention.

Walking over to his squad car, she greeted him with a smile and a chipper, "Hey, Uncle Alec. I was just about to call you about the council's new fuel emission rules."

But Alec looked grim. He tapped the side of the door. "Get in, Odelia."

"Why? What happened?"

"You better sit down for this."

With a puzzled frown, she got in and slammed the door closed. "What's going on?"

"Do you know this lady?" he asked, gesturing to the radio, where a song of Chickie Hay was playing.

"Sure. Who doesn't? She's only one of the most famous pop stars of the last decade."

"Well, now she's one of the most famous dead pop stars of the last decade," he said with a set look.

Odelia did a double take. "Chickie Hay died?"

"This morning. Her housekeeper found her. Strangled."

"Strangled!"

Uncle Alec nodded, tapping his fingers on the steering wheel. "I called Chase and he's going to meet us there. I want you on this one, Odelia, cause I have a feeling it's not going to be one of our easiest cases. And since she is what you just said she is, there's going to be a lot of scrutiny and a lot of pressure, you understand?"

Odelia nodded, still stunned by the terrible news. "Strangled," she repeated softly.

"Yeah, what a shame, right? I actually liked her music."

He stomped on the accelerator and the car peeled away from the curb. Soon they were zooming along the road. Odelia picked out her phone and decided to call her editor first. She had a feeling he wouldn't mind if she didn't show up for work, as long as she landed him the big scoop on who the murderer of Chickie Hay could possibly be.

"Maybe pick up your cats?" Uncle Alec suggested. "It's all paws on deck for this one."

She nodded as she waited for her call to connect.

Moments later she was back at the house, and she hopped out. "Yeah, hey, Dan. There's been a murder. Yeah, Chickie Hay. I'm heading over there now with my uncle." She opened the front door and yelled, "Max, Dooley, Harriet, Brutus! Got a job for you!"

As expected, Dan was over the moon, not exactly the kind of response a feeling fan or loving relative would like to see, but understandable from one who sells papers for a living.

Four cats came tripping into the hallway, all looking up at her expectantly. She crouched down. "There's been a murder," she said, without preamble, "and I need your help. Are you up for it?" They all nodded staunchly, and she smiled, doling out pets for her four pets. "Come on, then," she said. "Uncle Alec is taking us over there now."

Four cats hopped into the back of the pickup, and then they were mobile again, en route to Chickie Hay's no doubt humble abode.

The house was located in Hampton Cove itself, and not near the beach as most of these celebrity homes usually were. It wasn't a manor either, but a house that sat hidden behind a fence atop a modest hill. The only thing indicating this was no ordinary home was the gate you had to pass through. Uncle Alec pressed the intercom with a pudgy finger and held up his badge. The gate swung open and Odelia saw that the drive angled steeply up. Moments later they were surrounded by a perfectly manicured garden, and soon the car crested the hill and the house appeared. It was a large structure, painted a pastel pink and looking modern and cozy at the same time. Chase stood waiting for them, leaning against his pickup, and pushed himself off the hood when he saw them.

"Bad business," he said, giving Alec a clap on the shoulder and Odelia a quick kiss.

The four cats exited the car, then disappeared from view to do what they did best: interviewing pet witnesses and scoping out the place from their own, unique angle.

"Where is she?" asked Uncle Alec.

"Upstairs," said Chase, gesturing with his head to a large plate-glass window right over their heads. "She was rehearsing for her upcoming tour when it happened."

"No one saw anything?"

"I only got here five minutes ago so I figured I'd wait for you guys."

The woman who greeted them at the door was red-faced and very emotional. Judging from the way she was dressed she was perhaps the housekeeper who'd found Chickie, Odelia thought, and when she asked her the question, the woman nodded affirmatively.

"Yes, I found Miss Hay," she said. She was short and round, with a kind face and a lot of curly brown hair piled on top of her head. Her name was Hortense Harvey.

"Please show us," said Uncle Alec, adopting a fatherly tone.

"Did anyone come near the body?" asked Chase. When the woman uttered a quiet sob, he quickly apologized and corrected himself. "Did anyone come near Miss Hay?"

"No, detective. You told me over the phone not to allow anyone in so I locked the door—well, me and Tyson Wanicki, Miss Hay's bodyguard."

"Where was Mr. Wanicki when this happened?" asked Odelia.

"You will have to ask him yourself, I'm afraid," said Hortense. "I haven't been able to talk to anyone about what happened. I've been upstairs in my room crying."

Odelia decided to postpone the questions for later, when they had a chance to properly sit down with the woman. For now they needed to see what had happened.

Hortense led them up a staircase and into the upstairs hallway, then to the last door on the left, where a large man stood sentry. When they arrived, he nodded. With his bald pate, horn-rimmed glasses and white walrus mustache he looked more like a kindly uncle than a hardened security man. He definitely did not look like Kevin Costner.

The bodyguard answered in the affirmative when Uncle Alec asked if he was Tyson, and stepped aside so the trio could enter the room. It was a large room, one wall consisting of a giant mirror, not unlike the workout rooms in fitness clubs. Speakers were still blaring and on a giant screen a woman was going through some dance moves.

"You told me not to touch a thing so I didn't touch a thing," said Tyson. He darted a sad look at the lifeless body in front of the mirror, and a lone tear stole from his eye.

Uncle Alec placed an arm around his broad shoulders. "You better get out of here, Mr. Wanicki. But don't go too far. We want to have a word with you."

"Yes, Chief," said the man deferentially as he swiped at his teary face.

At the door, Hortense still stood, reluctant to enter. "You, too, Miss Harvey," said Alec.

"Yes, Chief Lip," said the woman, and the Chief closed the door behind them.

Once they were alone, he crouched down next to the body of the singer, shaking his head in dismay. "What a waste," he muttered.

Odelia's sneakered feet made a squeaking sound as she crossed the floor. The first thing that struck her was how small Chickie Hay looked. She also noticed the bruising on the famous singer's neck and the bulging eyes, a clear indication of how she'd died.

"You a fan?" asked Chase.

"Not a big fan, but I like her music, yeah," said Odelia.

"Me, too," said Chase, a little surprisingly. He was strictly a country and western guy, but then again, Chickie Hay had country roots, and her first albums had been all country.

Odelia glanced up at the video screen where the choreographer still stood showcasing complicated and exhausting-looking moves, and Odelia remembered she'd been going through a similar routine herself only an hour before.

"Abe will be here soon," said Uncle Alec, "but if you want you can start the interviews now. No sense in all of us waiting around for the big guy to show up, right?"

After one last look at Chickie, Odelia and Chase filed out of the room and saw that the bodyguard and the housekeeper had decided to wait outside. And as Hortense led them to a room where they could set up the interviews, Odelia wondered if Chickie had pets for her cats to interview. She hoped so, and she hoped they'd seen what had happened to their mistress.

3

I actually felt like the leader of the pack for once, as I moved along the greenery in the direction of the back of the house, three cats following my lead. It didn't last long, though, for soon Harriet fell into step beside me, scanning the grounds with her sharp eyes. "Our objective is to locate and interrogate any pets on the premises, Max," she said, then darted a stern-faced look over her shoulder at the others. "And that goes for you two, too. Keep your eyes peeled, boys—remember, Odelia is counting on us."

I heaved a deep sigh as she overtook me and then moved ahead of me, Brutus hurrying to keep up with her. Dooley and I fell behind and then lost sight of them.

"What is it, Max?" asked Dooley. "Why are you looking so sad all of a sudden?"

"For once I wish I were the one in charge—me being Odelia's cat and all."

"But you are the one in charge, Max."

"Tell that to Harriet. I'm sure she doesn't see it that way."

He gave me a reassuring smile. "To me you'll always be the one in charge, Max."

I have to tell you I was touched. It was one of the nicest things anyone has ever said to me. "Thanks, Dooley," I said. "That's very sweet of you to say."

"So what do we hope to find here, Max?"

"No idea. But you know what these ultra-rich celebrities are like. They like to keep some special pets no one else has. So we might expect a pet boa constrictor, a pet llama, a pet chimpanzee—anything goes."

"Got it," he said, looking appropriately serious for this most important mission.

"What do you think about Gran becoming the next Beyoncé?" I asked as we roamed around Chickie Hay's gorgeous garden, exotic plants covering every available surface.

"I'm not sure," he said. "You still haven't told me who this Beyoncé person is."

"Oh, right. Well, Beyoncé is—"

But unfortunately I was interrupted by the call of a bird. One glance told me it was a big bird—in fact a large peacock. And Harriet was already engaging it in conversation.

I resumed my instructive moment with Dooley. "So Beyoncé is—"

"What are you doing here?" asked a gruff voice in our immediate vicinity.

I glanced over and found myself locking eyes with a tiny French Bulldog.

"Oh, hi," I said. "My name is Max and this is Dooley, and we're here to—"

"Trespass, that's what you're doing," he barked. "Get lost, cats. This is private property."

"But—"

"No buts. Get lost now or I'm calling security."

"Oh," said Dooley. "I thought you were security, tiny dog."

The dog's expression darkened. "What did you just

call me?"

"Um? Security?"

"No, the other thing. Starts with a T and ends with Y. Horrible slur."

"Tiny dog?"

"That's the one. I'm going to have to punish you for that. Lie down and willingly submit to your punishment, cat. Come on, now. I'm going to give you one nip in the butt. And if you repeat the slur I'll have to give you two nips, so don't go there."

"But, tiny dog," said Dooley, "we're simply here because—"

"And you just had to go there, didn't you? Lie down and accept two nips in the butt." And he approached Dooley to administer the appropriate punishment.

But Dooley wasn't taking it lying down. He wasn't even taking it standing up. Instead, he said, "But, tiny dog, all we want is to—"

"And there you go again. Three nips is the proper punishment and you will take it like a cat, cat. Now face the other way. This will only take a second, and it will remind you not to repeat these horrible slurs to my freckled face."

"Look, tiny dog…" Dooley began.

"Four is the score! You're not the smartest cat in the litter, are you, cat? Four nips in the butt."

"Look, we're here to investigate the murder of Chickie Hay," I said. "So if you could tell us what you know we would be very much obli—"

"Murder?" asked the dog, expression darkening. "What are you talking about, cat?"

"Our human is a detective," I explained, "and she was called here to investigate the murder of Miss Hay. And as her pet sleuths we were hoping you could shed some light on the matter."

"This is crazy," said the doggie. "Chickie Hay is my human, and she's not dead. She's alive and kicking. Well, maybe not kicking, exactly, but singing and dancing. In fact she's right up there practicing for her new tour. And if you don't believe me just direct your attention yonder and you'll hear her angelic voice belting out her latest hit song."

We directed our attention yonder, as instructed, but I couldn't hear anyone belting out any song, new or old. In fact I didn't hear a thing, except for Harriet yapping a mile a minute to the peacock, who was looking slightly dazed from all this verbal diarrhea.

"Um? I don't hear anything," Dooley finally announced.

"Me neither," I said. "Are you sure she's up there?"

"Of course I'm sure," said the doggie, even though he now looked slightly worried.

The French Bulldog stared at us, clearly distraught, then, suddenly and without another word about nips in the butt, tripped off in the direction of the house.

"Not much of a witness," said Dooley. "He doesn't even know his human is dead."

"He could still prove a valuable witness," I said.

"He could?"

"He might not know what he knows and when we talk to him again, he might remember what it is that he didn't know he knew. If you know what I mean."

Dooley stared at me. "I'm not sure I got all that, Max."

I wasn't sure I got it myself. That's the trouble with being a detective: you just muck about for a while, hunting down clues, speaking to pets and people, and finally you may or may not happen upon a clue that may or may not be vital to the investigation. And if you're lucky you end up figuring out what happened. And if you're unlucky, well, then Harriet beats you to it by extracting the telling clue from a silly-looking big bird with spectacular plumage.

4

*L*aron Weskit sat enjoying his morning coffee whilst ensconced in front of the window of his hotel room. The room overlooked Hampton Cove's Main Street and as such was perhaps not the best room in the house for a man who valued his privacy, but still preferable to a view of the back streets of the small Hamptons town.

A buff young man with a fashionable buzz cut and a trim hipster beard, he was one of the youngest and most successful record executives, with several popular artists on his roster. He'd already scanned the business section of the *Wall Street Journal* on his phone and was just checking his emails when his smartphone sang out Charlie Dieber's latest smash hit. A good record executive plugs his clients any way he can, and adopting his protégé's hit song as his ringtone was but one way to accomplish this, subtly inflicting Charlie's latest earworm on whoever happened to be in the room with him.

"Tyson, my man!" he said. "Whaddya got for me, buddy?"

"Bad news, I'm afraid, Mr. Weskit," said Tyson.

"What is it this time? Another lawsuit? Or some fresh dig on Instagram?"

"I'm afraid Chickie's dead, Mr. Weskit."

For a moment Laron's brain ceased to function, as if incapable of grasping this plain truth. "Dead? What do you mean, dead?"

"She was murdered—strangled. Our housekeeper found her. Police are here now."

"So… do they know who did it?"

"I don't think so. The detectives just arrived, along with the chief of police. They talked to Hortense and I guess it'll be my turn next."

Laron thought hard. Chickie Hay dead. How was that even possible?

"So… about our arrangement, Mr. Weskit, sir?" said Chickie's bodyguard.

"What arrangement?" he grunted distractedly as he thought about the consequences of Chickie's unexpected and frankly shocking demise.

"Well… you said that if I kept you informed of Miss Hay's whereabouts and movements at all times I would be handsomely rewarded, Mr. Weskit, sir."

"You were supposed to be her bodyguard, Tyson," he said, suddenly experiencing a burst of irritation. "So why didn't you do your job and protect the woman?"

"I-I was downstairs in the kitchen, Mr. Weskit. Having breakfast."

"Some bodyguard you are. Having breakfast while your client is being strangled."

"She was rehearsing," said the man. "Said she didn't want to be disturbed. And there were plenty of people guarding the perimeter, so I'm pretty sure no one came in or out."

"So what are you saying? That it was an inside job?"

"I think so, sir."

"Yeah, well, I don't have any use for a bodyguard who allows his clients to die on his watch, Tyson. You understand what that's going to look like on your resume, don't you?"

"But, Mr. Weskit!"

"None of my clients will want to work with you. You know what pop stars are like, Tyson. Highly superstitious bunch. You're damaged goods now. Impossible to place."

"But, sir!"

"Maybe try the financial sector. Bankers are a lot less superstitious, or so I've heard."

And with these words he promptly disconnected. Best to sever all ties with the guy. Lest he wanted to look bad himself by being associated with a failed security man.

"Who was that, darling?" asked his wife Shannon as she strode into the room. Blond and impossibly skinny with an outrageously inflated bust, she'd managed to squeeze her perfect form into a sexy little red dress. Laron Weskit was not exactly a picture of male beauty, but what he lacked in physical attraction he made up for in business success, and since nothing turned Shannon on more than having a husband with several million in the bank, he'd been lucky enough to entice her to be his bride three years ago. Theirs was a happy partnership, based on one guiding principle: he made the money, and Shannon spent it. It made them both happy, and that's what a good marriage is all about.

"Chickie Hay is dead," said Laron, never one to beat about the bush.

Shannon's hand, which had been busy bringing a piece of avocado toast to her mouth, halted in midair, and she looked up, looking as shocked as he had been when Tyson had told him the terrible news. But she quickly recovered. "What happened?"

"Murdered. Police are on the scene. They don't know who did it yet." He directed an inquisitive look at his wife.

"You didn't happen to go out this morning, did you, darling?"

She laughed. "No, I didn't. You don't think I would kill the wretched girl, do you?"

"You never know. Chickie had a lot of enemies."

"And none more prominent than you," she pointed out.

"Yeah, I'm sure it won't be long before the police come knocking on our door."

"Why don't you call your friend the Mayor? I'm sure he'll be able to arrange something. Keep the baying hounds off our backs."

He smiled. That was Shannon for you. Always the practical one. "You're right. Why subject ourselves to scrutiny when we can avoid it? I'll make the call straight away."

"Too bad, though," said Shannon as she took a tentative nibble of her toast.

"Yeah, what a waste of talent."

"Not that. What a pity we don't have the rights to her new album. I'm sure it'll go triple platinum now."

"The value of her entire catalog will go through the roof. As it always does when an artist dies—especially a tragic death like this. Chickie's oeuvre will be a hot property."

Shannon held up her glass of freshly squeezed orange juice. "Here's to Chickie Hay. May she rest in peace—and make us a fortune."

"To a fortune," he said, loving how cynical Shannon was. And of course she was right. This murder business would make them even richer than they already were. That, unfortunately, was the nature of the business they were in. Or, as in their case, fortunately.

He got up, moved over to the connecting door and held up his hand, poised to knock.

"I wouldn't do that if I were you," said Shannon without turning.

"Oh? And why is that?"

"Young love, Laron. You remember what young love is like."

He retracted his hand. Shannon was right. "Still, they need to be told," he said.

"Later. Just let them rest. They'll find out soon enough."

"They should find out from me."

"And why is that? The news is what it is."

"Yeah, but I need to advise them on a media strategy before they touch their Insta."

"Call the Mayor. That's a better use of your time than bothering Charlie and Jamie."

5

*P*arked on one of Main Street's side streets, a good view of the Hampton Cove Star through the windshield of their rental, Jerry Vale and Johnny Carew sat watching the fourth-floor balcony of Hampton Cove's most prestigious and posh boutique hotel.

"Are you sure this is a good idea, Jer?" asked Johnny for the umpteenth time.

"Yeah, I'm sure, so stop whining, will you? My ears hurt from all your yapping."

"We just got out of jail, Jer," Johnny reminded his partner in crime. "And I don't want to go back there so soon."

"You won't go back, Johnny," Jerry growled. "This is a foolproof plan we're working on here. You know what fool-proof is? It means even a fool like you can't mess it up."

Johnny thought about this for a moment. "Are you saying I messed up the last plan?"

"You know you did. Who fired off that gun when he'd been told to be inconspicuous?"

"But you were under attack, Jer! I had to do something!"

"I was under attack from mice, Johnny. Mice! I was

dealing with it, but the moment you fired that big cannon of yours, you ruined everything."

They'd spent time in prison, until a nice judge had decided to let them out on bail, and now there they were, once again having decided to grant other, more prosperous members of society, the pleasure of carrying the burden of their livelihoods. This time Jerry had selected Laron Weskit and his client Charlie Dieber and Charlie's girlfriend.

"Do you realize Laron Weskit is the youngest, most successful record executive in the country? And that Charlie Dieber is one of the hottest pop singers in the world? These people are loaded! And we're simply going to take some of that load off their backs."

"I know, but Jer," said Johnny in the same whiny voice he'd employed ever since Jerry had told him about his plan to hit Laron and The Dieber. "They probably got security up the wazoo. So what if we get caught again? I don't want to get caught again, Jer."

"Listen carefully, cause I'm only going to repeat this once. Tonight the Mayor is organizing a party for Laron and The Dieber—Dieb is getting the keys to the city. So they'll all be downstairs, partying and having a ball, while we're upstairs, helping ourselves to their cash, jewelry, gold watches, and other precious little trinkets."

Johnny rubbed his chin at the prospect. It was a sizable chin, too, in proportion with the rest of his anatomy. Jerry, who looked more like something a cat dragged out of a dumpster, was, after all, the brains of their little outfit, while Johnny was the brawn.

"And what about Weskit and The Dieber's security people?"

"They'll all be in the ballroom protecting their charges, which means they won't bother us."

"I don't know, Jer," said Johnny, shaking his head and

showcasing an appalling lack of trust in his longtime companion.

"You don't have to know, Johnny," said Jerry. "I know, and that's enough."

Johnny nodded sheepishly. He knew he wasn't blessed with a big brain, and usually relied on his partner to supply that much-needed brainpower to carve out their criminal career. But Johnny didn't enjoy spending time in prison, and he was obviously loath to go back inside so soon after their last sojourn in the slammer.

"Just think about the diamonds, Johnny," said Jer, taking out his phone and calling up an image of The Dieber's girlfriend Jamie Borowiak, a nice big diamond necklace around her neck. He scrolled through the girl's Instagram some more and tapped the diamond ring Jamie had gotten from her boyfriend. In the next picture, a stunning pair of earrings. Switching to Charlie Dieber's Insta, there was a gorgeous gold watch on display and, finally, an entire collection of expensive-looking cufflinks on Weskit's Instagram. Jerry tapped the picture. "See these? Worth a fortune. And he takes them everywhere he goes."

"So nice of these stars to advertise their prized possessions on Instagram," Johnny said. "That way we know what to look for, going in." He might not like the prospect of venturing out into the line of fire again, but he did covet other people's wealth as much as the next crook. Finally he said, "Let's do this, Jer. When is this party?"

"Starts at nine, and goes on until after midnight, with speeches by the Mayor and the chairman of the local chamber of commerce and performances by Dieber and the girlfriend. Rumor has it there might even be some local talent infesting the stage. We hit the hotel at eleven, out by eleven thirty, tops. Plenty of time to become filthy rich."

"Filthy rich," Johnny repeated, his eyes sparkling. "I like filthy rich, Jer."

"Get used to the prospect. Cause tonight's the night. Nothing's gonna stop us now!"

❧

"*T*onight's the night," Tex spoke into his phone as he sat back in his chair. But then the buzzer buzzed and he jerked up. He checked the small screen that showed an image of the waiting room. When he saw Mrs. Baumgartner stalk in, he couldn't suppress a groan.

"Did you say something?" asked Denby Jennsen, his colleague over in Happy Bays.

"My receptionist took the day off again," he explained. "So now I'm supposed to handle all the phones and organize the flow of traffic in my waiting room all by myself."

"You really should start thinking about bringing in a professional receptionist, Tex," said Denby, not for the first time. "They do wonders for your peace of mind. And your productivity. I've had Vicky for ten years and I wouldn't know what to do without her."

"I know, but how can I fire Vesta? She's my wife's mother. Marge will never forgive me."

"I'm sure Marge will understand. And isn't your mother-in-law like, a hundred years old by now?"

"Seventy-five, and she still thinks she's hot stuff. She's launching a solo career."

Denby laughed. "A solo career! Doing what?"

"Well, singing, obviously. She wants to be the next Beyoncé."

"Tell her to go ahead. Maybe she'll be a hit and then you can finally hire a decent receptionist. You need one, Tex. You can't go on like this."

"I can, if only she'd come in for work every day."

He disconnected after admonishing Denby to be there tonight or be square, but before he let in his next patient, he took a moment. Denby had a point. A professional receptionist-slash-secretary would be great. Then again, he didn't pay Vesta all that much, what with her having room and board at the house and being family. She was more a glorified volunteer than an actual receptionist, and Tex had only given her the job because Marge wanted her mother to keep busy. To be around people. If he took that away from her, he'd deprive her of a big chunk of her social life. Plus, she probably wouldn't take it well, which might lead to more tensions at home, something to avoid.

Denby meant well, but he didn't fully grasp the situation. Best to leave things as they were. And so he walked over to the door and opened it, then plastered his best smile onto his face. "Mrs. Baumgartner? Come on in."

"Vesta not here today?" asked Mrs. Baumgartner, who was one of Tex's best patients—though Vesta claimed she simply carried a torch for him and that's why she was in all the time. He had to admit the woman had hypochondriacal tendencies. "So is she sick? Did something happen to her? I thought she looked under the weather when I saw her yesterday. Pale—and has she lost weight? She walked with a limp, too. Hip issues, probably. But then you would know best, wouldn't you? You are her doctor, aren't you?"

Great. Soon the whole town would think Vesta was knocking on death's door.

6

———

It was nice to be out in the garden. There were big exotic flowers everywhere, very colorful and very fragrant. And if I hadn't been given a very particular assignment, I probably would have wanted to spend the rest of the day there—or at least until my stomach told me it was time to look for greener, food-providing pastures. But as it was, we needed to find out who had murdered this nice singing person, so onward we went.

"Pity the little doggie didn't have a clue, right, Max?" said Dooley.

"Yeah, real pity," I agreed.

"Maybe Chickie has other, more observant pets?"

"I don't doubt it. She probably has a whole army of pets."

I was still eying Harriet and Brutus with a measure of pique. They seemed to have hit the jackpot when they stumbled upon that peacock. Sleuthing is a collaborative effort—a team sport, if you will—but Harriet and Brutus don't see it that way. They have this competitive streak that makes them view it as a competition sport instead. If they can manage to lay their paws on the telling clue, they won't hesitate to rub

35

my face in it. So I decided to go and look for a second peacock, hoping peacocks travel in pairs.

"We need to find peacock number two, Dooley," I said.

"Peacock number two? Who is peacock number two?"

"Where there's one peacock, there's bound to be a second one."

"You mean peacocks mate for life?"

"You tell me." Dooley had been watching a lot of the Discovery Channel lately, so if anyone had the inside scoop on these birds with the riotous plumage, it was him.

He thought for a moment. "I'm not sure, Max. Though I saw a documentary about hippopotamuses last week, and they don't mate for life, if that helps."

It didn't, but I decided to let it go. "Do peacocks sit in trees?" I muttered as I directed my eyes upwards to the foliage.

"Why are you so eager to find a second peacock, Max? We could ask Harriet what she learned from the first peacock."

"It doesn't work that way, Dooley," I said. "You know what Harriet and Brutus are like. They think this is all one big competition. They'll never let us near peacock number one, and they'll refuse to divulge the information the peacock has offered them."

"I don't know, Max. Brutus has changed. And so has Harriet. They're not as competitive as they used to be. I'm sure they all want us to work together now."

Just then, Harriet and Brutus passed us by. They were both looking extremely pleased with themselves. "So how is it going?" asked Harriet. "Not too well, I imagine?"

"We just discovered a Very Important Clue," said Brutus with a smirk. "A VIC, as they call it in our business. The Mother Of All Clues, or MOAC as we professionals like to say."

"It's going to break this case wide open," said Harriet.

"So what's the clue?" asked Dooley.

But Brutus mimicked locking his lips with a key and throwing it away.

Dooley stared at the gesture. "Why are you making those weird movements, Brutus?"

"It means his lips are locked," Harriet explained. "And so are mine."

"But… we're a team, right? We're all in this together."

"We're a team," said Harriet, gesturing between herself and Brutus. "And you're a team. And may the best team win."

"Let's talk to the peacock, Dooley," I said, turning away from the duo.

"He won't tell you a thing!" Harriet called out after me.

I turned back. "And why is that?"

"We made him sign a Nondisclosure Agreement," said Brutus. "An NDA as I call it."

"Everybody calls it an NDA, Brutus," I said. "And how can you make a peacock sign an NDA? You don't even have pen and paper."

"It's a figure of speech," said Harriet. "We told him not to tell you what he told us."

"But why?" asked Dooley, still looking puzzled by all this subterfuge.

"Why do you think? May the best cat win, Dooley."

"And get all the tasty kibble and gourmet food," Brutus added, licking his lips.

And then they were off, presumably in search of Odelia to deliver her the good news about the MOAC and the VIC, though perhaps not about the NDA.

After a moment, Dooley said, "Maybe you were right, Max. Maybe Brutus and Harriet haven't lost their competitive streak after all."

So we redoubled our efforts to find Peacock Number Two (or PNT). And I'd almost given up hope when we finally found it. PNT was strutting its stuff near a nice pond where I could see several fishes of exotic gillage flitting agilely through the water.

Any other cat would have stared at those fishes, eager to dip a paw in to try and catch one, but not me, and not Dooley. We're made of sterner stuff, and so we forewent the fishes and focused on the peacock instead.

"Hi, Mr. or Mrs. Peacock," I said as an introductory remark. "A word, please?"

The peacock rolled its beady little eyes. "Not again," it said. "I just told those other cats everything I know and I'm not going to say it a second time."

I was disappointed that this was not PNT but PNO. Still, I decided not to show it.

It's like that age-old advice when facing a predator: never show fear, because the predator will smell your fear and attack. When faced with a possible witness in a murder investigation the same principle applies: never show disappointment. Act as if you're one of those know-it-all detectives. Let nothing the potential witness says faze you.

"So where were you on the night of the fifteenth?" asked Dooley, who apparently had been watching too many cop shows recently, on top of his Discovery Channel binges.

"What my friend means to say is, where were you when Miss Hay was murdered?" I asked, hoping to break Harriet and Brutus's imposed NDA.

"Like I told your friends, I was right here, minding my own business, not getting involved in human affairs. Never get involved in human affairs," PNO admonished us.

"I'm sorry, but are you a he or a she?" asked Dooley, incapable of curbing his curiosity.

"First let me see some ID," said the peacock. "Who are you cats?"

"I'm Max, and this is Dooley," I said. "And I'm afraid we left our ID cards at home."

"I'm a he, and so is he," Dooley added, just to make matters crystal clear.

"In lieu of an ID we do have microchips implanted in our necks," I said. "So if you have a device capable of reading chips, you will be able to glean all there is to know about us, including but not limited to the name and address of our human and other valuable personal information."

"Okay, fine," said the big bird a little grumpily, "So what do you want to know? Oh, right, my gender. Well, if you must know, I find your question insulting. Why do I have to choose a gender? Why can't I simply be gender-fluid? Maybe today I feel like a girl, and tomorrow I feel like a boy. Why does society try to pin me down on one or the other?"

This momentarily rendered Dooley and me speechless, but my friend quickly recovered. That's what all that Discovery Channel watching does. It makes one resilient, and ready to take the vicissitudes of life and the animal kingdom in particular in stride.

"So what's your name, sir or lady?" he asked now.

The peacock shrugged. "Arnold," they said. "Or maybe Rose. Or Jasper. Or Francine. I consider myself name-fluid, which means that based on how I feel at any given moment I choose the name I like to use. And there's nothing you or society can do about it."

"Isn't that… a little confusing?" I asked, but the thunder-cloud that suddenly contorted the bird's face into an expression of displeasure told me I'd made another faux-pas.

"Maybe it's confusing to you, but that's probably because you're a fluidphobic bigot. And if you don't know what that means, I'll tell you. You, sir, are a hater of fluids."

"I think Max likes fluids," said Dooley. "Mainly water, though. Milk, not so much."

The bird raised itself to its full height, which was considerable, and already its ruffled feathers were starting to rise up. "Are you making fun of me? Is that what this is?"

I decided to try and defuse the situation. "So... it's Francine then, is it?" I asked.

"I feel like a Franklin right now, so call me Franklin," they said with a toss of the head.

"Great. So, Franklin, can you tell us anything pertaining to the murder of Chickie Hay who was, I presume, your human?"

"Never presume anything," said Franklin. "Just because she took me under her wing, and fed me and took care of me doesn't make her 'my' human."

"It doesn't?" asked Dooley.

"Of course not! That's such a paternalistic thing to say. She was my fellow living creature, and I loved and respected her, but that doesn't mean she was superior to me, or assumed a position of control over me. She was 'a' human but not 'my' human."

"Fine," I said, starting to find this conversation a little trying. "So what can you tell us about 'a' human named Chickie Hay and her recent demise?"

"She was nice," said the bird, momentarily looking off with a dreamy expression in their eyes. "She respected me as an individual, and never tried to impose the rigid strictures and structures of society on me. And only yesterday she had a big, great, giant row with her former best friend Jamie."

"Jamie Borowiak? The singer?" I asked.

"That's the one."

"What were they arguing about?"

"Boys, of course," said the peacock with a very expressive roll of the eyes. "What else? Jamie claimed that Chickie had tried to steal her boyfriend and Chickie claimed she'd known Charlie for so long the argument could be made that it was in fact Jamie who stole her boyfriend from her instead. It all ended with a big brawl and then Jamie stalked off and said she never wanted to clap eyes on Chickie ever again, and Chickie said that Jamie was dead to her and she hated her and hoped she choked and died." Franklin cocked an eyebrow at me. "But then Jamie returned this morning for a do-over of yesterday's fight, and this time she killed Chickie."

I was a little taken aback by this. "What, you actually witnessed the murder?"

"Not witness it, exactly. But I saw Jamie, and I heard her exchange heated words with Chickie in Chickie's dance studio. So my conclusion is that Jamie is Chickie's killer."

"Thank you, Franklin," I said, excited by this information. "That's very—"

"Um, the name is Immaculata," said the peacock. "The name just came to me."

"Well, thanks, Immaculata. The information is really—"

"Or better yet, call me Sookie."

"Thanks, Sookie."

"Or... how about Doogie?"

That was the moment we decided to part ways, before the name-challenged   Arnold-Rose-Jasper-Francine-Franklin-Immaculata-Sookie-Doogie drove us completely bananas.

hile Uncle Alec guarded the body and waited for the coroner to show up, Odelia and Chase had decided to tackle the interviews together. The first person they talked to was the housekeeper, as she'd been the one to find the singer. The room they'd been allocated was right next to the rehearsal space, and was a conference room, where Chickie probably conducted meetings with her team. On the wall several gold and platinum disks had been placed, along with plenty of posters of her successful tours.

Hortense was still visibly shaken by what had happened.

"Have you worked for Miss Hay long?" asked Chase, launching into the interview with a softball question.

"Oh, yes," the woman replied in the affirmative. "I've worked for her for seven, or maybe even eight years. Ever since she bought this house, in fact."

"Is this Miss Hay's primary residence?"

"Yes, it is. She's originally from California but she came on vacation here once and liked it so much she immediately bought the house and moved here with her family. She always said she found life more peaceful in Hampton Cove.

She also had a lot of meetings in town. Her record label is located in New York, and the recording studio, as well."

"What kind of person would you say Miss Hay was?" asked Odelia.

Hortense stifled a sob at the use of the past tense. "Very sweet, very kind, very loving. She was the kindest person I ever worked for. Always a hug and a kiss. She was more like family to me than an employer. I'm going to miss her terribly." She broke down in tears again and Chase fetched a box of Kleenex and placed it before her on the table. "What's going to happen to me now?" she asked between sobs. "What's going to become of me?"

"Didn't Miss Hay live with her mother?" asked Odelia. "Surely she'll keep you on."

"I don't think so, Miss Poole. Yuki never liked it here as much as Chickie did. Yuki—"

"Yuki is Chickie's mother?"

"Yes. Yuki Hay. She prefers LA. Always did. I'm sure she'll sell the house and return there soon after the funeral."

"Do you know if Chickie had any enemies?" asked Chase. "Anyone who meant her harm?"

Hortense shook her head. "No one," she said decidedly. "Chickie was so loving, so sweet—nobody could be enemies with her. She only had friends. Everybody loved her."

"But wasn't she recently locked in a conflict with her former record company owner?" asked Odelia. She was an avid reader of the gossip press and had read all the stories about Chickie having a very public falling-out with the man who'd discovered her.

"No, she didn't have a falling-out, simply a business disagreement. If anyone fell out, it's Mr. Weskit. Chickie had a big heart, and Mr. Weskit decided to take advantage of her, but Miss Hay didn't allow that to happen, and then Mr. Weskit came here last week and shouted a lot of abuse so he was kicked out. Chickie hated conflict—she hated getting into fights with people. But sometimes in this business you have to be strong, or else people walk all over you. So she was strong and Mr. Weskit didn't like it."

"What was the fight about?"

Hortense waved a hand. "Something to do with royalties. I don't know the details."

"Do you think Mr. Weskit can be violent if provoked?"

"I don't think so. His wife is another matter entirely, though."

"His wife?"

"Yes, Mrs. Weskit is a horrible person. I think she was very jealous of Miss Hay, and didn't like it when her husband and Miss Hay had such a good relationship, such a heartfelt connection, and so she tried to come between them, tried to break them apart, and she succeeded." The housekeeper nodded sternly as she pressed a Kleenex against her nose. "If there's anyone who is capable of murder it is certainly Shannon Weskit."

"Did she happen to drop by recently?" asked Chase, as Odelia jotted down the name.

"Yes, she was here," said Hortense, much to Odelia's surprise. "She was here the day after her husband was here, and she and Chickie argued. They argued very loudly."

"What were they arguing about?" asked Odelia.

"Laron, and how strongly Shannon felt Chickie should stay away from him."

"You could hear the argument?"

"Oh, yes. Like I said, they were very loud. Shannon said that if Chickie went near her husband ever again, she'd file charges for harassment, and Chickie said she was confusing a business relationship with a sexual relationship, and assured Shannon that she'd never felt about Laron Weskit that way. But Shannon said she didn't believe her for one second." Hortense pursed her lips disapprovingly. "And then she slapped her."

"Who slapped who?" asked Chase.

"I'm not sure, but I think Shannon slapped Chickie. At least when Shannon left I didn't notice any red marks on her cheeks, and Chickie looked furious, and she did have red cheeks. So I think it's obvious Shannon slapped Chickie, and the moment she left, Chickie turned to me and said, 'Make sure that woman never sets foot inside my house ever again.' So I assured her I'd tell Tyson, and then Chickie returned to her room upstairs, where she always writes her new songs, and for the rest of the afternoon she didn't come down again. She just sat there playing her guitar. I felt very bad for her."

"When was this?" asked Chase.

"Yesterday afternoon," said Hortense with a nod of certainty. "She only came out again when Jamie Borowiak dropped by in the evening and they sat in the garden."

"Jamie Borowiak?"

"She's Chickie's best friend. Or at least she was, until Jamie got involved with Charlie Dieber, who went and ruined everything for them. But that's a different story." She gave them an eager look. "Do you want me to tell you that story, too?"

They both nodded. "Yes," said Chase. "We want you to tell us everything you know."

The woman smiled. "Oh, I know a lot. There's no secrets in this house for me."

And Odelia had the impression she was proud of the fact, too.

8

_W_e were making our way back to the house, in search of Odelia so we could tell her the information we'd gleaned from the gender-and-name-fluid peacock, when we found ourselves waylaid by the tiny French Bulldog who came streaking out of the house.

"She's dead!" he cried, clearly distraught. "You were right, cats. My human is dead!"

"I'm so sorry," I said.

"I went up there to see how she was, but there was a large cop walking around and when he slipped out the door for a moment I slipped in and there she was. Not moving!"

"I'm afraid she was murdered," I said. "Which is why we're here—to find out who did this to her."

"But… they have to call an ambulance! Maybe she can still be saved!"

"She's been dead for quite a while now," I said. "I'm afraid it's too late to save her."

"There must be something they can do! With all the advances in science—can't they try something experimental? Something new and untried?"

"What experimental thing?" asked Dooley, interested.

"I don't know!" said the doggie, flapping his ears. "There has to be something they can do, right? Like when I had this terrible pain in my tail, and the vet fixed it."

"I'm afraid that once you're dead, that's it," I said, hating to be the bearer of bad news, and probably risking a nip in the butt, or possibly even two. "Nobody can fix dead."

The doggie sank onto his haunches and then burst into a bout of honest tears. "Oh, no," he said. "My human. Dead. This isn't happening!"

"It is happening, actually," said Dooley.

"Dooley," I said, and shook my head to indicate he should probably exact restraint in a moment fraught with sadness like this.

"She wouldn't leave me," said the doggie. "She said she'd always be there for me."

"She didn't leave you," said Dooley. "She was murdered. You can't help being murdered."

"Dooley," I repeated, and shook my head again. We needed to tread very carefully.

"Murdered!" said the doggie. "But who would do such a thing?"

"That's what we're here to find out," I said. "And we were hoping you could help us in our investigation."

He sniffed some more, looking distinctly miserable. "I have no idea. Who would harm such a loving, warm, sweet, wonderful person like Chickie? She was a goddess. She was perfection. She was God's angel. Everybody loved her. Everybody and especially meeee!"

"Well, she must have had enemies. Otherwise she wouldn't have been killed so tragically."

"I'm telling you, she had no enemies. Angels don't have enemies. She brought only sweetness and light into this world and we all loved her. Adored her—worshipped her!"

"So… what about this Jamie Borowiak person who dropped by yesterday and again this morning and got into a flaming row with Chickie both times?"

"Jamie was Chickie's best friend in all the world. She would never get into a flaming row with her. Never. They organized slumber parties. They sang together. They recorded songs for each other's albums and they performed shows together. They would never get into a fight. And Jamie would most definitely never murder her best friend."

"We talked to Doogie just now," I said.

"Who?" asked the dog, a confused frown on his face.

"The peacock," said Dooley. "They said their name might be Immaculata, though, or even Sookie. It's a little confusing."

"Oh, you mean Mark. Yeah, don't listen to Mark. He used to belong to a rapper, and I think all that rap music must have affected his brain. It got scrambled a little. Or a lot."

"What's your name, by the way?" asked Dooley.

"Boyce Catt," said the French Bulldog. "Don't laugh. Chickie wanted a dog and Yuki—that's her mother—wanted a cat. So Chickie called me Boyce and Yuki called me Catt."

"Well, Boyce Catt," I said, "Mark told us that Jamie was here yesterday and she and Chickie sat out in the garden and got into a big fight. Jamie accused Chickie of trying to steal her boyfriend Charlie Dieber, and then she stalked off on a huff."

"But she came back this morning to do some more fighting," Dooley added.

"That's true," said the doggie. "I saw her. They made up, though."

"They did?"

"I was there when Jamie dropped by this morning. She walked in when Chickie was rehearsing in the dance studio.

There was a moment of name-calling but then they decided they loved each other too much to fight over a silly thing like a boy and they hugged and made up."

"They hugged?" I asked.

"Yes, they did. And I ask you, is that the behavior of a would-be killer?"

"Jamie could have been pretending."

"She would never do that," said Boyce Catt. "Jamie and Chickie have been besties for years. Also, Chickie was the sweetest person alive. No one could hold a grudge against her. Absolutely no one, and most definitely not her best friend." He sniffled a bit more, then frowned and said, "You want to know what I think happened? I think this is a case of mistaken identity. Has to be. Someone killed Chickie thinking she was someone else. Or maybe a burglary gone wrong. Someone broke into the house to steal Chickie's valuables and she happened to be in the wrong place at the wrong time."

"It's possible," I allowed.

Frankly anything was possible. We had no clue what had happened, exactly, and the burglary gone wrong thing had happened before, especially when the victim was as rich as Chickie.

"Let's find Odelia," I told Dooley. "We have a lot to tell her."

"Thank you so much, little doggie," said Dooley, and it was an indication of Boyce Catt's mournful mood that he didn't even suggest nipping Dooley in the butt again. Having your human suddenly snatched away from you by the grim reaper has that effect.

And we'd just set foot for the house when a big and burly male came walking out. He was talking into his phone, saying, "Please, Mr. Weskit, sir. You have to help me. You promised, Mr. Weskit, sir," and then he passed out into the garden as we passed into the house like ships in the night. Or, more precisely, two cats and one human in the daytime.

$\mathcal{T}$he next person to join Odelia and Chase was Chickie's sister Nickie. She took one look at the conference room and wrinkled her nose. "Mama and I would like to talk to you but not in here. Mama hates this room. In fact Mama hates every single room in this house except for her own, so if you could talk to us in there, she'd be very much obliged."

And since Chase and Odelia were most interested in talking to Chickie's nearest and dearest and didn't care where the interview was conducted, they followed Nickie Hay out of the room and along the corridor, then up a flight of stairs to the next floor.

Odelia noticed how Chickie's sister wore house socks of a very colorful and thick design, and was otherwise dressed in plain jeans and a sweater. She looked very much like her sister, only with brown hair instead of blond, but otherwise the same fine-boned face and cupid's bow mouth.

Nickie was carrying a Starbucks coffee mug in her hand, but didn't offer any refreshments to Chase or his civilian consultant. Once upstairs, she swiftly moved to the first door on the right, and when it swung open it was almost as if they'd entered a different world. The room was airy and bright, with lots of paintings adorning the walls: small little paintings of boats and seascapes. The color scheme was navy blue and white and seagulls dotted the wallpaper. On the coffee table a large book of paintings by Renoir lay, and in a wicker chair overlooking the garden sat Chickie and Nickie's mom. She was fair-haired and slender and had large eyes. She'd tucked her feet underneath her and watched as Odelia and Chase took seats on a sofa, Nickie preferring to remain standing.

"Terrible news," were the woman's opening words. "Absolutely devastating."

She didn't look all that devastated to Odelia, though.

"So what have you found out?" asked Yuki Hay. "Who is responsible for my daughter's murder? And have you talked to Tyson and asked him how he could have let this happen?"

"So far we've only talked to your housekeeper Hortense, ma'am," said Chase.

"Oh, please don't 'ma'am' me," said the woman with a light chuckle. "Call me Yuki."

"Chase Kingsley, Yuki. And this is Odelia Poole."

"Pleasure," said Yuki. "Though you'll agree that the circumstances are not ideal."

"Mom, don't be so callous," said Nickie.

"I'm not being callous. The circumstances are terrible, that's a fact. Now have you offered these nice police people something to drink?"

"No, I haven't," said the young woman, clearly having no intention of offering them anything while she took another sip from her own cup.

"What can I get you?" asked Yuki, directing an annoyed glare at her daughter.

"We're fine," said Chase.

"Nonsense. I'm not suggesting you have a stiff whiskey, though I could sure use one." She got up and walked over to the liquor cabinet, which, Odelia saw, was well stocked.

"Why don't I pour myself something, and call down for Hortense to bring up some refreshments?"

"Really, Yuki," said Odelia. "There's no need."

"Poppycock," said the woman, and poured herself a liberal helping of an amber liquid, then picked up her phone and said, "Hortense, please bring the nice detectives something to drink. Tea? Coffee?" she asked, turning to Odelia with an inquisitive look.

"Coffee is fine," said Odelia, and Chase nodded that he could do with the brew, too.

Moments later Yuki Hay was seated again, sipping from her liquor, and judging from the twin red circles that appeared on her cheeks it was hitting the spot just fine.

"Did your daughter have any enemies?" Odelia asked.

"Where do you want us to start?" said Nickie.

"You simply can't get where Chickie got in this business without creating a bunch of enemies in the process, Detective," said Yuki. "So along the way to success the road is littered with disgruntled business partners, musicians, producers, record company executives, competitors, ex-boyfriends and whatnot. The list is endless, and we don't even know the names of half these people. Success breeds jealousy, and jealousy makes people do strange and horrible things. Luckily Chickie never really got entangled with any of that stuff. She wasn't one to bear a grudge." When her daughter made a scoffing sound, she looked up in surprise. "Well, she wasn't, Nickie."

"Oh, yes, she was. Chickie could bear a grudge as well as the next diva. And she loved it. She collected grudges and feuds like other people collect shoes or stamps. She even kept notebooks with her grudges so she would remember where she left off."

"Any of these people happen to be around?" asked Odelia.

"Well, I heard Charlie Dieber is in town. And then there's Laron Weskit and his wife. And if I'm not mistaken Jamie Borowiak was in here yesterday, getting into another big screaming row with Chickie."

"Jamie was here?" asked her mother. "Why didn't she come up to say hi?"

"Because she and Chickie haven't been on friendly terms for a long time."

"I didn't know. Why didn't anyone tell me? I could have talked some sense into them."

"Because Chickie loved her fights and had no intention of being talked out of them. Besides, I didn't even know about most of her feuds, to be honest. Nor did I care."

"You worked as your sister's personal assistant?" asked Odelia.

"Yes, that's right. She only trusted family, so I took over as her PA a couple of years ago."

"And you've done such a wonderful job, too," said Yuki. "Chickie wouldn't be where she is today if it wasn't for..." She paused, then corrected herself. "Chickie wouldn't have been where she was without her twin sister."

"You're twins?" asked Chase.

"Not identical ones," said Nickie, "but yes, Chickie was my twin."

"Why did she only want to work with family?"

"Because the PA she had before me was a liar and a thief."

"She stole from us," said Yuki. "Used her expense account to buy Louboutins and Louis Vuitton purses and even two iPhones—one for herself and one for her mother."

"Don't forget about the Netflix account she bought her cousin in Connecticut or the Lexus she got for her dad."

"Chickie was always too naive, and too generous," said her mother.

"She wasn't naive or generous," said Nickie. "She was swindled."

"Did you go to the police?" asked Chase.

"Yes, we did. The woman did a couple of months of hard time and was ordered to pay back the money she stole. People who work for a person of such extreme wealth as my sister are sometimes tempted by all that opulence. They think what's thine is mine and start spending money without thinking. When I found out I told my sister and the woman's contract was immediately terminated and charges filed."

"How did you find out?" asked Odelia.

"Before I was my sister's assistant I was her accountant."

"Nickie has a degree in economics," said her mother. "She even has an MBA, isn't that right, darling?"

"I have an MBA," Nickie confirmed. "I worked for Ernst & Young for a while, until Chickie asked me to join the family firm as her personal accountant. She was doing so well it seemed like a pity not to enter the fold."

"Her previous accountant swindled her out of a million dollars," said Yuki.

"Jeezes," said Chase. "Is there anyone who didn't swindle your daughter?"

"That's exactly why she decided only to work with family," said Yuki.

"Dad works as our accountant now," said Nickie. "He's a CPA."

"And what did you do for your daughter, Yuki?" asked Odelia.

"Oh, I worked as her stylist. That's my profession, you see. I used to design clothes for a living."

"And she was very good at it, too," said her daughter.

"Oh, nonsense," said the woman modestly. "I worked for

Oscar de la Renta for a long time, but when Chickie needed me, of course I hopped at the chance."

"So how many family members worked for your daughter, Yuki?" asked Chase.

"Um… let me think. Well, cousin Greg, of course. He's our impresario—in charge of everything to do with Chickie's tours and concerts. Cousin Sam organizes the car park and the fleet of private jets. Cousin Mimi takes care of the houses —we have a place in LA, a pied-à-terre in Paris, an apartment in London, and of course Lake Cuomo. Mimi does a wonderful job keeping them all in tip-top shape and making sure they're ready when they need to be. She's also in charge of hiring and firing all household staff."

"And you all live together?" asked Odelia, surprised.

"Yes, we all live here," said Yuki, "though Mimi is on holiday right now."

"And Sam is in France," said Nickie, "checking out a new jet."

"And Greg is in Manhattan, talking to tour promoters about the US tour."

"And cousin Martine—she's our PR person—is in London setting up a video shoot."

"We'll have to call them," said Nickie. "They'll have to come back for the funeral."

Mother and daughter were silent for a moment as they contemplated the reality of the situation: the family firm had just lost its raisin d'être—its shining star.

"I called your father just now," said Yuki finally. "He was devastated, of course. He's flying home immediately."

Chase handed Yuki a piece of paper and a pen. "Could you make us a list of the people present at the house this morning, Yuki? We would like to set up interviews with all of them."

"Oh, sure," she said.

"So why is there only a small crew here right now?" asked Odelia.

"Chickie was rehearsing for a tour, and writing new songs," said Yuki.

"My sister loved to be surrounded by her family and friends, but not when she was in creative mode. Then she liked to be alone—let inspiration be her guide."

"Once she had a couple of songs written, or an idea of how she wanted the new tour to look like, the house would be buzzing again." Yuki's shoulders sagged a little. "Only now the house will never buzz again, will it? Not without my little girl at its heart."

10

*M*arge was just wondering if she hadn't forgotten something when the doorbell rang again. She rolled her eyes and yelled, "Ma! Someone here to see you!"

A wild guess, but one she was pretty sure was correct.

The doorbell had already sung out five times that morning, every time announcing one of her mother's admirers. When Mom didn't respond, Marge stomped into the hallway and yanked open the door, only to find yet another pensioner on the mat.

The man flashed a set of perfectly bleached pearly whites and she forced a smile onto her own face.

"Hi there, Marge," said the man.

"Hi there, Dick. I'll bet you're here to see my mom?"

"Unless you're prepared to be my lady of the night," he quipped.

"Ha ha," she laughed without much enthusiasm. "I think I'll leave that honor to my mother." She stepped aside. "She's in the basement."

"Oh, a secret meeting in the basement, huh? Now isn't that exciting?"

Dick Bernstein was one of Gran's oldest friends, and a regular at the senior center. Mom had told her he was a great dancer, though Marge doubted whether that was why she'd invited him over today.

When the sound of people talking floated up from the basement, Dick said, "I recognize a great party when I hear one. Sounds pretty cozy, Marge—you sure you don't want to join us?"

"Very sure," she said, and as she watched him potter off in the direction of the basement door, hoped the old man wouldn't break his neck on those rickety stairs.

She wondered what her mother was up to now, but was afraid to ask. First Tex had turned the basement into a rehearsal space for him and his two doctor friends. Together they were The Singing Doctors, and they were actually pretty good. They played jazz with Tex on vocals, Denby on drums and Cary Horsfield on guitar. They'd soon shaken up the lineup, though, when it turned out Tex couldn't sing. Now Denby was the frontman, Tex played drums, and Cary still rocked the guitar. They were looking for a trumpet player but so far no other doctor had responded to their request to join the band.

Ma had quickly shown a keen interest in The Singing Doctors and had volunteered as backing vocalist. And to Marge's amazement it had worked out pretty well. Tex and Mom had called a truce, and for the first time in years they'd actually gotten along.

And now this. Ma launching a solo career, with the assistance of her senior center buddies. She just hoped the new Beyoncé would keep things PC down there.

*O*delia had just stepped out into the garden to get some fresh air when she bumped into Max and Dooley.

"Odelia!" said Max. "We've been looking for you!"

She quickly glanced around to see if anyone could overhear them, then asked, "So what did you find out so far?"

"Well, for one thing," Max said, "Chickie's former best friend Jamie Borowiak dropped by the house yesterday, and they had a flaming row about Chickie allegedly trying to steal Jamie's boyfriend away from her."

"Charlie Dieber?"

"Yes, that's the one," said Max.

"And this morning," said Dooley, "Jamie came back, and she and Chickie made up."

"Though we only have Chickie's dog Boyce Catt's word for that," said Max.

"What else?" she said.

"Well, we just overheard a big man talk to someone named Weskit on the phone. He was talking about a promise Mr. Weskit made him, and sounded pretty desperate."

"What did this big man look like?"

"He had no hair on top of his head and a very nice white mustache," said Dooley.

Odelia nodded. "Tyson Wanicki and Laron Weskit. Who would have thought?"

"Oh, and Harriet claims she cracked the case," said Max, "but she refused to tell us how. So you'll have to ask her what she found out."

"She talked to the same big bird we did, though," said Dooley, "so chances are that Mark—that's the big bird's name —told her the same thing he told us."

"About Jamie and Chickie having a big fight over Charlie Dieber," Max clarified.

"Great job, you guys," Odelia said as she pressed kisses on top of her cats' heads. And as she straightened, she caught sight of Tyson as he stood smoking a cigarette on the deck. She quickly made a beeline for the security man.

"Tyson? Can I have a quick word?"

"Sure, Miss Poole."

"So we've talked to Hortense, and also to Yuki and Nickie, and so far the picture I have of what happened this morning is becoming a little clearer. And I was hoping you'd be able to confirm certain details."

"Of course," he said. "Whatever you need."

"So Jamie was here early this morning? And she and Chickie met in the dance studio?"

"That's correct. Jamie is one of Chickie's oldest friends, and she always got access to her. Though this morning Chickie didn't seem very happy when I ushered Jamie in."

"They had a fight yesterday," Odelia explained.

"Oh, right. That would explain the frosty reception."

"When did Jamie leave?"

"Um, just after six, I would say."

"And Chickie was still alive at that time?"

"Yes, she was. I saw her myself. She told me she didn't want to be disturbed."

"And did anyone else drop by after Jamie left?"

"Nobody."

"So where were you when Chickie was holed up in her studio?"

"In the kitchen, having breakfast," he said, looking a little embarrassed.

"How many security people were watching the Hay family this morning?"

"Um, there's a crew of five."

"And you're the person in charge?"

"Yes. I tell them where to go and what to watch out for.

The house has a top-of-the-line security system. No one gets in or out without being seen. We have motion sensors and security cameras. Also, two people walk the perimeter, keeping their eyes peeled."

"So… correct me if I'm wrong…"

"Yes, Miss Poole?"

"No one came into the house after Jamie left. And the house was so well-guarded you would have noticed if anyone did."

"Yes, that's correct."

"And yet Chickie was killed somewhere between…"

"The last time I saw her was at six thirty."

"And Hortense found her at seven. So she was killed between six thirty and seven."

The man nodded.

"So this must be an inside job, no question about it."

"Yes," Tyson agreed. "Someone who was already in the house must have killed her."

"And only you were here, and your team, and Nickie, Yuki, Hortense…"

"And half a dozen staff."

She gave the man a pointed look. "You do realize you've just incriminated yourself, don't you, Tyson?"

"Oh, no, Miss Poole. I would never do anything to harm Miss Hay."

"Is it true you've been in contact with Laron Weskit recently, Tyson?"

His eyes went wide and he stammered for a moment, but then finally cast down his eyes. "Yes, Miss Poole. Yes, I have."

_I_t was our opportunity to listen in on a real-live interrogation and we weren't going to miss it for the world. Odelia was grilling a potential killer. Dooley and I sat around, casually being inconspicuous, while Odelia asked this bodyguard a couple of zingers.

"Is this what a detective does, Max?" asked Dooley, and I confirmed that this was exactly what a detective did, which, in a sense, Odelia was and more.

"Laron Weskit contacted me last year," said Tyson. He'd lit up another cigarette and was taking a long, fortifying drag. "He and Chickie had fallen out by then and she was in search of a new record company, ready to sign a contract for her next couple of albums. Laron needed someone on the inside, and asked me to be his eyes and ears."

"He wanted you to spy on Chickie."

"Yes, that's what it boiled down to. He said Chickie had abandoned him, and it was only a matter of time before she did the same to me."

"Did she have a history of dumping business associates, or members of staff?"

"Not that I was aware of. Most people left after working for her for a while. Chickie was a perfectionist, and if you didn't do things exactly the way she liked, she could really haul you over the coals. So I knew Laron had a point. Sooner or later I'd make a mistake and it would be my ass on the line. So I decided to take him up on his offer."

"Which was?"

"If I kept him informed of which record companies Chickie was in contact with, and the state of the negotiations, he'd recommend me to the stars he had under contract."

"Do you think Laron is the kind of man capable of murder?" she asked.

"I doubt it. Laron is a businessman, not a killer."

"Yes, but we all know what happens when an artist dies, Tyson."

He looked puzzled. "I don't..."

"The value of their catalog goes up. And Laron Weskit owns the rights to all of Chickie's old songs, doesn't he?"

"He does," the man confirmed.

"It's a strong motive for murder, Tyson. Was Chickie's new album ready?"

"I... I'm not sure. Chickie was very secretive about it. She didn't confide in a lot of people. Not even her own family. Only last week Yuki complained she hadn't heard the new songs yet."

"Who had heard those new songs?"

"Um, just the producer, I guess."

"Is he here?"

"No, he's in New York. Chickie has been coming and going to his studio for the past couple of months. I know because I'm the one who's been driving her."

Odelia smiled. "Tell me honestly, Tyson—you *have* heard

the new songs, haven't you? And you've been secretly recording them and sending them to Laron Weskit."

"No! I would never do that, Miss Poole. You have to believe me. All I did was keep an eye on the record executives Chickie was in negotiation with. Laron was still hoping to reach an understanding with her. Make a new deal. He wanted to know if he still had a chance. These big players have deep pockets, and he wasn't sure he'd be able to keep up."

"Is Laron in town?"

"Yes, he and his wife are staying at the Hampton Cove Star. Charlie Dieber, who's under contract with Laron, is being offered some kind of award. Keys to the city."

"So Charlie and Laron are both staying at the Star," said Odelia pensively.

"I guess so."

Odelia nodded, and I could tell what she was thinking: time to pay a visit to Laron and Charlie, and find out what they'd been up to.

"One last question," she said.

"Yes, Miss Poole."

"Can you definitely rule out the possibility that an intruder managed to get past security and murder your employer?"

He stared at her for a moment, then heaved a deep sigh. "No. I know I should probably lie and tell you such a contingency is out of the question, but that's not the case. Theoretically there's always a chance someone managed to sneak in unseen and out again, killing Miss Hay in the process. But the chance of that happening is very slim."

"But there is a chance?"

"There's always a chance, yes, whatever any security expert might tell you."

Odelia returned indoors while the bodyguard stayed

rooted in place, eagerly drawing from his cigarette. The man had just admitted something he probably shouldn't have.

"If this is true, anyone could have come in and murdered Chickie," said Dooley.

"Yes, any old prowler could have killed her," I agreed.

And then a strange sound reached my ears. It seemed to come from the other side of the house. And as Dooley and I went in search of its source, we were met by Harriet and Brutus, who'd noticed the same thing. It came from across the fence, so Dooley quickly scaled it, followed by Brutus and Harriet. The only one who wasn't scaling it was me.

Look, I've lost weight recently. A lot of weight. To the extent that I now fit through the pet flap again. But that still doesn't make me the skinniest cat on the planet—the kind of cat that scales fences with effortless ease.

"What's going on?" I yelled to my three friends.

"Come up here and see for yourself!" Harriet yelled back.

I stared at the fence. It was conveniently covered in ivy and looked scalable. So I took a deep breath, and put my first paw on the ivy, then slowly but gradually moved up until I'd reached my friends. And I was so over the moon with my heroic effort that I almost didn't notice the strange young man who stood singing a famous Chickie song below us. He was also lobbing long-stemmed red roses over the fence for some strange reason.

And just when I thought he'd go away, he walked up to the gate and started banging it with his fists, then started actually crawling up the sturdy thing!

It swung open, though, and soon three burly men descended upon him and grabbed him. And then Chase joined them and before the man could utter another bar of the Chickie Hay song, he'd been cuffed and escorted in. The gate closed, and soon all was quiet again. And when I glanced around, I understood why all was so quiet: I was alone up there on that fence. And down below, Harriet, Brutus and Dooley sat staring up at me.

"What are you doing still doing up there, Max?" asked Harriet. "Get down here!"

Easier said than done. I had absolutely no idea how to get down from my perch.

*T*he experience wasn't new to me. Usually my bugaboos are tops of trees, or roofs of houses, but the fence was a novelty. Still, it boiled down to the same thing: I was stuck.

I could have jumped, of course, considering the nine lives things and all, but that fence was easily six feet high, and I've never harbored a death wish in my life.

"Max! Get down!" Dooley encouraged me.

"I can't!" I shouted back. "I'm stuck!"

"Don't talk nonsense, Max," said Brutus. "Just get down here."

"Funny, isn't it!" I replied.

"What is?"

"Usually the two of us are stuck together!"

He chuckled. "You're right. That is funny."

Or maybe not.

"I guess we better ask Chase to get you down," said Harriet with a sigh of annoyance.

"Oh, no, please don't," I said.

"Why? What do you have against Chase?"

"Nothing. I'm just embarrassed that he keeps having to save me."

"You can't stay up there, Max," Harriet pointed out with infallible logic.

"What's going on?" asked Mark the Peacock as he came prancing up.

"Max is stuck on top of your fence," Brutus explained. "He can't get down."

"What are you doing there, cat?!" the peacock shouted.

"Taking in the view, Mark," I shouted back.

"Who's this Mark you're talking about?"

"I thought your name was Mark?"

"My name is Hannibal," he said. "But my friends all call me Hanny."

"Well, Hanny, if you have an idea how to get a cat down from a fence…" said Harriet.

"Let me give it some thought," said Hanny. And he wandered off to exercise his little gray cells.

Next was the little doggie. "What's Max doing up there?" he asked.

"Hi, Boyce Catt!" I said. "I need a ladder. Can you help me out?"

"I'll see what I can do," said Boyce Catt, and went off in search of a ladder.

"This is silly," said Harriet. "Chase will happily get you down from there. Chase!" she shouted, and disappeared before I could stop her.

"Now that there's no chance of you blabbing about it, I don't mind revealing who killed Chickie Hay," said Brutus. He paused for effect, then said, "It was Jamie Borowiak."

"According to our information she and Chickie made peace this morning," said Dooley. "And Chickie's bodyguard says Chickie was alive after Jamie left."

"Shoot," said Brutus. "And here I thought we'd cracked the case."

"The case remains uncracked," Dooley said. "But Odelia has a lead. She thinks a man named Laron Weskit might have done it. So there's that."

"Did you give her that lead?"

"I guess we did."

"Again, shoot," said Brutus. "Harriet won't like this."

"Why is she so competitive about this?" I asked from my position on top of the fence.

"Oh, I don't know. She feels she should be the number one sleuth, mainly because she's a girl, and Odelia is a girl, and Gran is a girl, and then it's all girls together, see?"

"No, I don't see," said Dooley, and frankly I didn't see it either.

"So they can be a team. Harriet, Odelia and Gran. Like Charlie's Angels? Three girls fighting crime. Harriet saw the movie and now she wants to be the third angel."

"Why?" asked Dooley, clearly puzzled.

"I'm not sure. She says it's feminism."

"So who's Charlie?" asked Dooley.

"Some old, rich guy," said Brutus.

"So feminism is an old, rich guy who tells three women what to do?"

"I guess. You better ask Harriet, though. She knows all about it." He stretched. "Anyway, I guess our work here is done, so it's back to the homestead for us."

"Odelia and Chase are still busy figuring things out, though."

"They don't need us to do that, Dooley."

"I think they do."

"Listen to me, Dooley," said Brutus, placing a brotherly paw on Dooley's shoulder. "There's a point when we cats stop being useful to our humans. A point where they say

'Thank you very much, cats, but we'll take it from here.' And this is just such a point."

"I'm not sure, Brutus," said Dooley. "I don't think we ever stop being useful."

"I don't care what you think, I'm getting out of here. All these dead bodies and weird peacocks giving us faulty clues are seriously freaking me out." And then he was off.

"Do you want me to come up there and keep you company, Max?" asked Dooley.

"Nah, I'm fine, Dooley."

"Do you want me to get you some food? You'll starve to death up there."

"I don't think I'll be up here that long. Or at least I hope not."

"What we need is a fire engine. With one of those nice firemen to help you down."

"No need," I assured him. "The solution will come to me. I just need to think really hard for a moment—really think this through—and the answer will pop into my head."

And as I started thinking hard, suddenly an ambulance came driving up, followed by a black sedan. The black sedan was Abe Cornwall's, the county coroner, and the ambulance was there to pick up the body of the unfortunate Chickie. The gate swung open, and sedan and ambulance zoomed through.

And as they did, Dooley suddenly yelled, "Jump, Max! Jump!"

"What?"

"Jump on top of that ambulance!"

Clearly Dooley had had a brainwave. And so I jumped.

13

"We caught this guy scaling the gate," said Chase as he pointed in the direction of a skinny youth with pink hair. They were back in the conference room, their ad hoc command center. Odelia stared at the kid. With his effeminate features and lots of makeup it was hard to be sure whether he was a guy or a girl, actually.

"I was just trying to get close to my soulmate!" cried the kid.

"And who might your soulmate be?" asked Chase.

"Chickie, of course."

Uncle Alec had also joined them, after being informed Abe had finally arrived.

"What's your name, son?" the Chief asked.

"Chickie Hay," said the kid.

"What a coincidence," said Chase with an eyeroll.

"Your name is Olaf Poley," said Chase, having had the perspicacity to dig out the kid's wallet.

"I'm having it officially changed to Chickie Hay next month," said the kid. "I filed the petition so it's only a matter of time before I'll share a name with my soulmate."

He looked a little like Chickie, Odelia had to admit. Fine-boned features. Cupid's bow lips. He was a lot younger, though, and a boy.

"Are you related to Chickie?" she asked now.

"Of course I'm related! Didn't you hear a word I said? I'm her soulmate! We were put on this earth to be together forever. I can even sing like her. Do you want to hear?" And before they could stop him he'd burst into song. He didn't sing all that bad either.

Tyson walked in, took one look at the kid and groaned. "Not again."

"Hi, Tyson," said the kid happily. "Say hi to Chickie for me, will you?"

"Do you know this guy?" asked Uncle Alec.

"Yeah, we filed a restraining order against him last year. I think it still stands. You're not allowed within a hundred yards of Chickie, you know that, right?" he asked, sternly addressing the young man.

"I'm sure Chickie doesn't know about the restraining order. You filed that just to keep us apart. She waved at me this morning. So I know it's her entourage that wants me out of her life, not Chickie. An entourage, I might add, that's jealous of the bond we share."

"He's Chickie's most persistent and annoying stalker," said Tyson.

"She had more than one?" asked Odelia.

"Yeah, she had plenty, but this one takes the cake. Can't keep him away."

"Because we're soulmates," the kid repeated in a sing-songy voice.

"Do you think he could be the person we're looking for?" asked Uncle Alec.

"Of course I'm the one," said the kid with a little curtsy.

"The one who killed her, I mean," Uncle Alec said.

The kid stared at the chief of police, his jaw dropping so precipitously Odelia had the impression it was going to fall off.

"Wait, what?" Olaf said, suddenly adopting a normal tone.

"I think he could be," said Tyson. "He's crazy enough."

"Take a seat," said Uncle Alec, and gestured to a chair.

"No, but wait," said the kid. "What did you just say?"

"Sit. Down," the chief growled, and pushed Olaf down onto a chair.

Faced with two police officers, Odelia and Tyson, Olaf suddenly was a lot less cocky.

"Chickie is… dead?" he asked in a small voice.

"You know perfectly well that Chickie is dead," growled Uncle Alec. "You killed her."

"What? No! You–you're kidding, right? Chickie is fine and you're just joshing me."

"Do I look like I'm joshing you?" asked Uncle Alec, his face a thundercloud. "Where were you between six thirty and seven this morning?"

"I–I was out there," he said, pointing to the window.

"Out where? Be specific, Olaf."

"Out there by the fence, waving at Chickie."

"So you waved at Chickie and then you jumped the fence."

"No! I'm allergic to ivy so I would never jump that fence. Eww."

"It's just ivy, Olaf, not poison ivy," said Tyson. "So there's no way you're allergic."

"So you didn't scale the fence, go into the house, and murder Chickie," said Chase. "Is that what you're saying?"

"Yes! Yes, that's exactly what I'm saying!"

They all stared at the pink-haired kid for a moment. He was the perfect suspect, Odelia thought. He was obviously obsessed with Chickie, and he'd already proved he could scale the gate. Still, it was hard to prove he was the one they were looking for. First they would need some more information from Abe. Fingerprints, maybe, or DNA.

"Arrest him," said Uncle Alec.

"Wait, what?!" said the kid, now looking distinctly terrified.

"I think you did it," said Uncle Alec. "I think you're exactly the kind of creep who would do such a horrible thing and I don't want to risk you fleeing the scene. Get him out of my face," he told Chase.

"Wait, I didn't do anything!" said the kid. "I didn't do it, I swear! Tyson, you have to believe me. You know I would never harm Chickie. Never! I'm her biggest fan!"

"And her soulmate, yeah, we get it," said Alec. He got up into the kid's face. "You did it, Olaf. And I'm going to prove it."

14

---

*T*he good news was that I'd managed to get off the fence. The bad news? I was on top of an ambulance which, as we all know, is like a big box on wheels. So I was still stuck.

Suddenly a voice rang out behind me. "Hey, Max!"

"Dooley!" I said when the familiar figure of my friend gracefully dropped down next to me. "What are you doing here?"

"I'm keeping you company until someone can take you down."

"But... you shouldn't be up here, Dooley," I said, even though I was touched by the gesture.

"Harriet and Brutus have gone in to tell Odelia, so it's only a matter of time before help arrives. So I thought I might as well come up here."

I traced the route my friend had followed: he'd climbed a tree, then hopscotched across an overhanging branch and hopped onto the ambulance like a feline Tarzan. "Well done," I said admiringly. "Well done indeed."

"Thanks, Max. Nice view from up here." I followed his

gaze and had to admit the view was nothing to cavil about. Cats like to seek out high places where they have a perfect overview of their surroundings and we got all that and more.

"The only thing that's missing is food," I said. I'd secretly hoped to catch a bite to eat from Boyce Catt's food bowl but instead found myself on top of a food-less ambulance.

The ambulance stood parked in front of the house, and soon two of Abe's people came walking out, carrying a stretcher on which a form was placed covered with a sheet.

"Chickie," said Dooley softly as we stared down at her inert form.

"Yeah, Chickie," I confirmed. "Poor woman. She could sing like an angel, and now her voice will forever be silent."

The stretcher was placed inside the ambulance and the doors slammed shut.

"This is our opportunity, Dooley," I said, and so we both opened our throats and meowed up a storm to attract the attention of the two paramedics. Unfortunately, they either didn't hear us or chose to ignore us. At any rate, suddenly the ambulance lurched into motion, and we were on the move!

"Max!" Dooley cried. "We're moving!"

"I know!"

"I don't like this!"

"Me neither!"

The ambulance gained speed, even as we hollered up a storm. No one was listening, though, and soon we were zipping through the gate and then the ambulance really picked up speed and was racing away from Chickie's house at a fast clip.

"Where are they taking us?" asked Dooley.

"Hauppauge," I said. "That's where the county coroner's offices are located."

"But I don't want to go to Hauppauge, Max! I don't even know where Hauppauge is!"

"Me neither!"

So we both hunkered down on top of the roof, and as the wind played through our manes and our ears were flattened against our heads, I reflected this was definitely not the most pleasant adventure I'd ever participated in.

Odelia had told us to help her figure out who had killed Chickie, but this was taking our zeal for the case a little too far: we were actually escorting her body to the coroner!

"Odelia will come and get us!" I shouted to Dooley over the noise of the wind.

"I hope so!" he shouted back. "It's much nicer inside a car than outside, Max!"

"I know!"

"I don't know why dogs like this so much!"

"Me neither!"

It was true what he said. Dogs love to stick their heads out of windows of driving cars. Why, I don't know. To feel the wind tugging at you is not a pleasant sensation at all.

It felt like hours before the ambulance finally slowed down and entered the parking lot of a squat white building that looked like a space ship.

"I think we've arrived," I said.

"I hope they have food," said Dooley. "I'm hungry from the trip."

"I doubt they'll have food for us here, Dooley."

The ambulance drove into a garage bay and then came to a stop. The paramedics hopped out and opened the doors. This time they carried Chickie off to God knows where, and soon we were left in that garage, not a soul in sight.

"Look, Max," said Dooley, gesturing to a car that stood parked right next to the ambulance. It was only a short jump from the roof of the ambulance to the roof of the other car, and only a short jump to the hood of the car and then to the garage floor.

"I feel very strongly we should stay put," I said. "Otherwise Odelia will never be able to find us."

"Or we could go home on paw."

"It's a long walk back to Hampton Cove."

For a moment, we stayed on top of that roof, but then one of the coroner's people came walking up to the ambulance, got in, and started up the engine.

"Now or never, Dooley!" I cried, and we made the jump. Just in time, for the ambulance peeled out of the bay, probably to pick up more dead people.

And that's how we found ourselves on the concrete floor of the garage of the medical examiner's office, with no plan of where to go or how to get out of our predicament.

"I suggest we hang around here," I said. "Odelia will come and find us sooner or later."

So we hunkered down and decided to wait for our savior to show up.

"It's not very nice in here," said Dooley after a while.

"No, it's not."

It was a garage, and looked like any garage: all concrete and very smelly.

"Let's go and find us something to eat," I finally said, making a decision.

"But I thought you said we needed to stay put?"

"Yeah, but it will take Odelia a while to find us, and in the meantime we might as well eat. This place is full of humans. And wherever humans are, there's food to be found."

"Especially considering how big Abe is," said Dooley. "He must need a lot of food."

Abe Cornwall is the county coroner and looks as if at some point he swallowed another county coroner. The man is large. And since large people like to stay large, they need a constant supply of fatty and starchy foods. And since we just lived through a very harrowing adventure I felt I urgently needed to get my paws on some of Abe's stash.

We soon found ourselves in a series of long and sterile-looking corridors, all white walls and concrete floors. Just like a hospital—or a veterinarian's office. Yuck.

"I don't like this place, Max," Dooley intimated. "It's not very cozy."

We wandered here and there, and finally became aware of the sound of voices. They came from a large room that reminded me even more of a hospital, complete with an operating table at its center. And on that operating table lay... Chickie Hay!

"Max, what are they doing to her!" Dooley cried.

"Don't look, Dooley! Cover your eyes!"

"They're operating on her, Max, even though she's dead!"

The sight was so upsetting we decided to flee the scene, and soon found ourselves in yet another room, this time a very cold one. The door behind us slammed shut and as I glanced around I had the impression that all those white sheets on all of those metal tables were covering something that could only be...

"Dead people!" Dooley cried as he caught sight of one person without a sheet.

And as the truth came home to me that we were surrounded by dead people from all sides, my appetite suddenly went right out the window. I was hungry no more!

"This place is full of dead people, Max!" cried Dooley.

"I know, Dooley!"

"I don't like it!"

"I don't like it, either!"

Unfortunately the door was shut, and so we were pretty much stuck in there. I might mention that it was also very cold in there—freezing cold, in fact.

"Scream, Dooley," I said. "We need to get out of here."

And so scream we did. We meowed, we yowled, we mewed, and we screamed up a storm. Before long, a human person, a live one, yanked open the door and when he saw us scratched his head and muttered, "Well, I'll be damned." Then he shouted, "Abe! There's two cats in the freezer!"

Abe came waddling up and when he saw us frowned deeply.

"Those are Odelia Poole's cats," he said. "How did they get in there?"

"Max!" Dooley cried. "He's got blood… on his hands!"

And so he had. Abe's gloved hands were covered in blood, and so was his apron. In fact he looked more like a butcher than a doctor!

So we both screamed some more.

"Call Odelia," said Abe. "Tell her that her cats somehow got shipped back here."

"Probably hitched a ride with the body," said the man who'd opened the door for us.

"Yeah, probably." He chuckled freely. "Funny."

I didn't think it was all that funny, though. Not funny at all.

"Take them in the kitchen," Abe instructed. "And give them some milk, will you?"

And so the guy picked us both up and carried us out of the horrible dead people freezer. He took us into a kitchen, where it was warm and didn't smell like a hospital, and gave us a saucer of milk, and a couple of slices of liverwurst. And by the time Odelia finally showed up, we'd both settled down a little from our most terrifying ordeal.

"Oh, my sweet pets," she said as she knelt down. "What happened to you guys, huh?"

"I got stuck on top of an ambulance," I said.

"And I kept him company," said Dooley.

"And then we suddenly found ourselves in a room full of dead people."

"And Abe with his hands full of blood."

"And Chickie on an operating table."

"So horrible!"

"I know, I know," she said. "Let's get you guys home, shall we?"

She brought us back to her car and we happily jumped in. To our surprise, Harriet and Brutus sat waiting for us in the backseat. Before Odelia closed the door, though, she said, "Let me just check something. I'll be back in a sec." And stalked off.

After a moment, Dooley said, "She's probably gone to get us some more liverwurst."

15

It had been a long time since Odelia had set foot inside the medical examiner's office, and she did so with a sense of unease. The clinical feel of the place did little to encourage her to venture into its inner sanctum: the operating room where Abe conducted his autopsies. He was a dedicated professional and actually enjoyed his work, which she found both admirable and a little hard to fathom. Cutting open dead people seemed like a strange way to make a living. Then again, to each their own, of course.

She found Abe as he removed his plastic gloves. He was humming a little tune. His assistants, meanwhile, returned Chickie to a semblance of good form for the funeral.

"And?" she asked, deciding to ignore the work in progress lest she lose the bagel she'd eaten while driving over here for her urgent cat rescue operation.

"Oh, hey, Odelia," said Abe as he glanced up. He walked into his office and gestured for her to follow him. The office was a mess, documents strewn about, his desk piled high with work-related files. He sat back for a moment as he frowned. "Um… you're here for…"

"Chickie Hay? The woman you just examined?"

"Oh, that's right," he said, snapping his fingers. "Chickie Hay. Well, as I suspected she died from strangulation. And the person didn't use a cord or a rope or anything like that." He held up his hands instead, and wiggled his fingers. "He or she used this."

Odelia gulped. "Anything on the perpetrator?"

"Nothing yet, except that they must have really hated Chickie. Strangulation usually indicates a personal motive. The killer has to get in there, up close and personal."

"So was it a he or a she? I mean, you can probably tell from the size of the hands?"

But Abe shook his head. He wasn't going to allow himself to be pinned down. "I'm sorry. Could be a man. Could be a woman. I can't tell you with absolute certainty, Odelia."

She sank down onto a chair. "Incredible. Usually we don't have any suspects and in this case we have too many."

"Hasn't your uncle made an arrest?"

"Yes, but I'm not entirely convinced he's the person we're looking for."

"Looks like you've got your work cut out for you, then. What about your cats? Are they all right?"

"Yeah, they're fine. They must have been dozing on top of the ambulance when it took off."

He chuckled. "Funny little creatures." He lifted his hands. "Well, if there's nothing else, I need to write my report. Your uncle is waiting, and I'll bet a great deal of other people are, too. She was quite the celebrity, wasn't she, this, um…" He frowned.

"Chickie Hay."

His face cleared. "That's right. Chickie Hay. I'm not into her style of music, I have to confess. Pop singer, was she? I'm more of a jazz man myself. This pop music…" He indicated a hand flying right over his head to show her what he thought of pop music. "Here today, gone tomorrow, whereas jazz will always survive the test of time, whether its performers are alive or have been dead for years. Now that's real music for you."

She got up. "Thanks, Abe, for giving me the scoop on this."

"Oh, that's all right. I know you're not one of those annoying reporters who are always ready to screw up an investigation by printing stuff they have no right to. Well, good luck with your investigation, and let me know what you find."

"Will, do, Abe," she said, and raised a hand in farewell before leaving the office.

This case was quickly proving a real head scratcher. Usually they had a limited number of suspects but in this case they seemed to multiply the longer she worked on it. There was Laron Weskit and his wife Shannon, Charlie Dieber and his girlfriend Jamie, Nickie Hay and Yuki Hay, Hortense, Tyson, Olaf Poley, and a dozen others, members of Chickie's staff and security team. And then there was the worrisome fact that anyone could have scaled the fence that morning and snuck into the house to commit murder.

For a person who was as universally beloved and popular as Chickie Hay, the pop star had collected a surprising number of enemies.

What she needed to do, Odelia thought as she reached the car, was make a list of all possible suspects and their motives. Maybe then she'd finally start making some progress.

She got into the car and turned to the four cats anxiously waiting in the backseat.

"And?" she said. "What have you guys discovered so far?"

"Not much," said Max.

"Except that a coroner's office smells like a hospital," said

Dooley, "and that it's full of dead people kept in a very big freezer."

"I'm sorry you had to see that."

"But where do all these dead people come from?" asked Harriet.

Clearly Max and Dooley had been regaling the others with the story of their eventful trip.

"This is the medical examiner's office for the entire county," Odelia explained, "so all the suspicious deaths, all the suicides, and all the murders are brought here to be examined. And if you know that nine hundred autopsies are performed in Suffolk County every year, you can imagine Abe and his team have their hands full processing them."

"Creepy," said Brutus, who looked a little freaked out.

"Yes, it's a very particular profession," said Odelia, turning back to face the front and inserting her key into the ignition, "and personally I don't have the stomach for it."

"Me neither," said Max. "I wouldn't want to do what Abe does. No way."

"Well, that probably goes for a lot of professions out there," she said as she started up the car and put it in gear. "There's lots of people who wouldn't want to be a doctor, or a baker, or a plumber, or a painter. That's why it's important to choose a profession you know you're passionate about. Like me. I love being a reporter. It's more than just a job for me. It's something I enjoy, and would probably even do if no one paid me to do it."

"So what professions do you advise for us to take, Odelia?" asked Harriet.

"Um..."

"I'll start," she said. "When I grow up I want to be a singer. Like Celine Dion. And tour the world with my band, and play in big arenas for thousands of people. I think I'm an entertainer at heart, and I think people would pay good money to watch me perform. Your turn, Brutus. What do you want to be?"

"Uh..." said Brutus, who clearly had never given this a moment's thought. "I guess... I could come and watch your show?" he said tentatively.

She slapped him on the paw. "That's not a job, silly. You could do my backing vocals, though. All good artists have people to do their backing vocals and you could do mine. That way we get to travel together on my tour bus and fly around the world on my jet."

"Yeah, I'd like that," said Brutus, scratching his nose. He didn't seem overly excited about the prospect of singing backing vocals. Not for Harriet or anyone else.

Odelia had swerved out of the garage and was now cruising along the highway.

"What about you, Max?" asked Harriet, who clearly loved this game. "What is your greatest passion?"

"Well, I love to eat," said Max. "Especially now, being safe and sound and on my way home, I suddenly feel very hungry."

Harriet grimaced. "Max, you're not paying attention. We're talking about the kind of work we want to do when we grow up. A job that is aligned with your greatest passion."

"But I'm already grown up," said Max, "and so are you, Harriet. And since we're cats and not humans we don't need a job. We have humans looking after us, and providing us with food and shelter and love and affection. The only job I see myself conceivably getting passionate about is helping Odelia solve the occasional mystery, which I already do now. But apart from that I don't have a job, I don't need a job, and I don't want a job."

"I'm disappointed in you, Max," said Harriet, making a face. "I thought you were a cat who was going places, like me and Brutus. But instead you're simply another deadbeat.

Shame on you." She now turned to Dooley. "What about you, Dooley? And don't tell me your ambition in life is to eat, too."

"Oh, no," said Dooley. "I also like to drink. It's very important to stay hydrated. And sleep, of course. It's very important to get plenty of rest."

"Oh, Dooley,'" said Harriet with a shake of the head. "Looks like you've got two deadbeats on your team, Odelia. I'd say cut them loose and replace them with cats that show some spunk. A sense of initiative. But I know what you're going to say: you can't simply kick out Max and Dooley. And you're probably right, from a charitable point of view, but at least try to talk some sense into them. Try to make them see that there's more to life than eating, sleeping and drinking, will you? Because frankly it's frustrating for two ambitious cats like myself and Brutus to have to deal with this nonsense."

And after this long harangue, she lapsed into silence, causing Odelia to smile before herself and wisely keep her tongue.

16

"How much longer is it, Jer?"

Jerry checked his watch. "Well, the party starts at nine. The show starts with a performance by some unknown local artists, and The Dieber and Jamie Borowiak are scheduled to perform at eleven, so that's when we're going to hit their rooms."

"Are you sure the coast will be clear? What about security?"

"I told you a hundred times already—security will be downstairs, protecting the stars, not their rooms."

"And how do you know all this, Jer?" asked Johnny, looking slightly mollified.

"Let's just say a little birdie told me. And that same little birdie also told me we can expect a very nice haul. A very nice haul indeed," he added with a wide grin.

"I'll bet that little birdie wants a cut of that haul, though, right?"

"Little birdies always want a cut of the haul, Johnny. You know that."

Johnny was shaking his head again, looking anxious. "I

have a bad feeling about this, Jer. And the last time I had a bad feeling about a job and we went ahead and did it anyway, I almost got shot and we both spent the rest of the month in the slammer."

"You won't spend a minute in the slammer this time," said Jerry, patting his friend on the back. "I've got it all worked out. There isn't a contingency I haven't considered, and no risk that I haven't eradicated. This is the most lucrative, easiest job we'll ever pull, buddy. Just you wait and see."

"I don't know, Jer," said Johnny, looking particularly dubious.

"Well, I do, so just trust me and get ready to rake in the dough."

Jerry settled back as he thought about this dough they were about to rake in. It wasn't every day they were hitting several multi-millionaires in one go. It was the opportunity of a lifetime. Walk in, collect the loot, and walk out. Easy peasy. He smiled as he thought about it. This was going to be the most laid-back job they'd ever pulled!

He thought about his ex-wife Marlene. If he offered her a couple of diamond rings, a few necklaces, and one or two priceless bracelets, she might consider taking him back. And it was with a head filled with roseate hopes and dreams that he crossed his arms, dropped his chin on his chest, and dozed off.

෨

*W*hen Tex arrived home, he was surprised by the terrible racket rising up from the basement. It almost sounded like... a party. In his own basement!

So he set foot on the first step, and quickly descended the stairs. Much to his surprise about half a dozen senior citizens of the male persuasion stood gathered around Vesta, shooting the breeze, glasses of what looked like bubbly in their hands.

"What's going on here?" he asked, a frown on his brow. Vesta, who seemed to be the center of attention, greeted him by raising the glass of bubbly in her own hand.

"Great news, Tex," she said. "I've been selected as a last-minute addition to the show."

"Show? What show?"

"Some shindig for a couple of the Mayor's buddies. Plenty of bigwigs and celebs."

"You mean the Charlie Dieber thing? But I'm playing that —with my band."

"I know. What a coincidence, huh? We're sharing the stage. Marge will be so thrilled. She's always going on and on about the two of us being buddies, and now we'll be able to give her a show from the same stage." She held up her finger. "Hey. I just got an idea. Why don't we sing a duet, you and me? Our bands can join us, yours and mine."

"But… you're part of my band!"

"Not anymore I'm not. Didn't you get the memo? I'm going solo—with my own band." And she gestured to the elderly men, who all stood nodding enthusiastically. And since all of them were Tex's patients he couldn't even freak out in front of them.

"But, but, but…" he sputtered.

"All this singing I've done for your Singing Doctors have given me a taste for the stage. I'm the kind of woman who craves the limelight. I need to be center stage, not tucked away somewhere in the back going *Ooh-wah doopee dooh*. I'm a star, not a minion."

"It was my idea actually, Tex," said one of the men whom Tex recognized as Dick Bernstein. He was a distinguished-looking gentleman, with a full head of neatly coiffed white hair and a gorgeous little mustache. He was dressed, like the other pensioners, in a nice white tux. "Talent has to shine, and supreme talent must shine supremely." He directed an affectionate look at Vesta, who patted his cheek appreciatively.

"Yeah, Vesta's talent is so vast Dick told her to go solo," added a second gentleman. This was Rock Horowitz, also one of Gran's friends, and possibly an old boyfriend, too.

The others now all murmured their assent. "Vesta was made for the stage," another older gentleman agreed. "She has the voice, the presence, the looks. She's a born star."

"He's right, you know," said Dick. "Vesta was born a star, and it's a surprise to me why she waited this long to shine."

"No hard feelings, Tex?" asked Vesta. "I'm sure you'll find some other ninny to sing backing vocals for you. After all, anyone can be a backing vocalist. Not everyone can be the star of the show like me."

"But... what are you going to sing?" asked Tex, still recovering from the shock.

"Oh, you don't have to worry your little head about that," said Vesta with a dismissive gesture of the hand. "You just focus on your stuff and I'll focus on mine."

"With all due respect, Vesta," said Rock. "I think this idea of you and Tex performing a duet is a dud."

"I agree," said Dick, actually twirling his mustache. "A star like you needs to be discerning. I'm sorry to have to say this, Tex, but you and your singing doctors suck."

"I didn't want to say it, Tex, but Dick is right," said Vesta. "You're simply not good enough yet. Maybe you should practice a little more before you go on stage again."

"Not everyone is a natural like Vesta," Rock agreed.

"If you perform a duet now you'll only drag her down," said Dick.

"And you don't want to drag down a real star, do you, Tex?"

"Do you, Tex?"

"Um… no, I guess not," said Tex, his head spinning a little at this turn of events.

"Great," said Dick, giving him a thousand-watt smile, his gleaming white teeth practically blinding Tex.

"Excellent," Rock agreed.

"See? What did I tell you, Vesta?" said Dick. "I told you Tex would see reason."

"Yeah, I told you he'd let you go once he realized how talented you were."

"Thanks, Tex," said Vesta now, giving Tex a cursory hug. "I know it's hard for you to let me go, but I need to spread my wings and fly. And now buzz off, will ya? I need to practice." And she raised her glass of Tex's best champagne to her lips and drained it.

As Tex stumbled out of the basement he felt a little sandbagged. Had he just witnessed one of those *A Star is Born* moments? Was his mother-in-law going to be the Lady Gaga in this story and Rock and Dick her Bradley Coopers? Hard to believe.

17

"*W*hat do you mean we can't come near them?" asked Odelia.

She was in her uncle's office, discussing the case with the Chief and Chase, and the Chief had just dropped a bombshell.

"We can't talk to them," said Uncle Alec, fiddling with an empty pack of cigarettes. "At least not until after the show tonight."

"The Mayor's orders," said Chase, looking as annoyed as his superior officer. "He doesn't want his guests of honor bothered over this murder business."

"But… we *have* to talk to them. Jamie is a suspect, and so are Weskit and his wife."

"I'm sorry," the Chief grumbled, clearly displeased. "My hands are tied."

"So are mine," said Chase.

"Well, mine aren't," said Odelia. "And I'm going to talk to these people."

"Odelia, don't," said her uncle. "The Mayor isn't going to be happy if he finds out you disobeyed a direct order."

"I don't work for the Mayor! He doesn't get to order me around."

"Fine," said Uncle Alec. "But don't say I didn't warn you. If he hears about this, he'll—"

"He'll do what? He can't do a thing about it. Not a thing."

"He can talk to Dan, and he can lean on him. Make your life difficult."

"Why is this so important anyway? Who is this Laron person to the Mayor?"

"The Mayor is giving Charlie Dieber the keys to the city. He's hoping it will attract a lot of attention. The kind of attention a town that caters to the tourist crowd wants. And poking around and trying to associate Charlie and his girl-friend, or indeed the Weskits, with Chickie Hay's murder is bad for business. So he wants the investigation conducted quietly. Discreetly. And most of all he doesn't want Charlie being interrogated by the police on the night he's being awarded the keys to the city from the hands of the Mayor."

"Fine," said Odelia, rolling her eyes. "So all we have to do is wait until tomorrow and we're in the clear?" She didn't want to cause trouble for her uncle and Chase, or indeed Dan. And it wasn't as if the Weskits or Charlie and Jamie would skip town all of a sudden. They were all famous figures and famous figures have a much harder time laying low.

"Oh, sure. Tomorrow we can interview them as much as we want. Just not tonight."

"Okay, then. So where are we so far?" asked Chase, giving Odelia a wink.

"Not very far," said the Chief. "We talked to everyone involved, except the foursome currently holed up at the Hampton Cove Star, and we're not much the wiser for it."

"We did make an arrest," Chase reminded him. "We have young Olaf behind bars."

"Pretty sure young Olaf is innocent," grumbled Odelia's uncle. "I spent two hours grilling the kid and nothing. My gut feeling is that he's got nothing to do with this."

"So let's list them up," said Odelia. "Tyson was being paid by Laron Weskit to spy on Chickie. Find out what record companies she was talking to."

"But would he kill her over that?" asked Chase. "Not likely. Tyson is a security guy, taking money from Weskit, but he had no motive whatsoever to murder Chickie."

"He did say she could be tough to work for."

"Yes, but that doesn't mean he was going to kill her," the Chief pointed out.

"No, you're right. It takes a lot more than being a demanding employer to make people want to wring your neck," said Odelia. "So who else do we have?"

"I made a list of all the people on staff," said Uncle Alec, tapping a piece of paper on his desk. "These are the people who were in the house at the time of the murder, and so all of them could theoretically have killed Chickie."

"Long list?" asked Odelia.

"Too long," Uncle Alec grumbled. "Cooks, maids, security, gardener, assistants… About a dozen people in all."

"This is a nightmare. Plenty of suspects but nothing conclusive. And no witnesses."

"As I said, though, not much of a motive," said Chase. "These people might not have liked their employer, but there's not a single one among them with a criminal record."

"What about the family?"

"Only the mother and the sister were at the house this morning," said Uncle Alec.

"Motive?"

"Not one that I can see," said Chase. "Both mother and sister were dependent on Chickie's success. With her gone, the goose that lays the golden eggs is also gone, and even though they probably stand to inherit a fortune, that money will run out."

"Her death is likely to generate an enormous income stream, though," said Odelia.

"In the short term, yes, but not in the long run. And why would Yuki kill her own daughter? Or Nickie kill her sister? I don't see a motive, do you?"

Odelia shook her head. She didn't see a motive there, either.

"Moving on, we have Jamie Borowiak. And we have Shannon Weskit."

"Both have motive and Jamie definitely had opportunity. She was there that morning, and could have come back. And Shannon Weskit could have snuck in unseen."

"Apparently anyone could have snuck in unseen," Uncle Alec grumbled.

"What about the coroner's report?" asked Odelia. "Anything that stands out?"

"Nothing," said the Chief, sagging a little. "No fingerprints, no DNA—at least not so far. Almost as if our mystery killer is a ghost." He sighed. "Where are the days when a killer would leave a nice footprint right outside the window? Or a set of fingerprints?"

"All the bad guys watch CSI nowadays," said Chase.

Odelia and Chase got up as if on cue. "I need to start working on my article," she said.

"Are your cats all right?" asked Chase.

"Oh, yes, they're fine. A little shook up, but nothing a bowl of kibble won't fix."

"They didn't find anything either, I assume?" asked Uncle Alec.

"Apart from that clue about Jamie and the fact that the bodyguard was in touch with Laron Weskit, nothing so far," she admitted.

"Well, at least it's more than what we found," said Chase.

"Tell them to keep digging," said Uncle Alec. "They've come through for us before, and I have a feeling we're going to need every helping paw we can get." He laughed at his own joke. "Get it? Lend a helping *paw*?" When no laughter ensued, he shook his grizzled head. "Kids these days. No sense of humor."

18

*O*delia had dropped us off at the house before racing off again, and frankly I was happy to be home. This sleuthing business can be fun, but today it had taken a lot out of me, and I couldn't really be bothered to find out who had killed whom, to be honest.

The first thing I did was eat my fill, then I proceeded to this week's favorite spot, and as I made myself comfortable on the windowsill, which offers a great view of what goes on out in the street, I heaved a contented sigh and finally started to feel like myself again.

Dooley had joined me—plenty of space on the sill—and was smiling benignly.

"Maybe our purpose in life is simply to nap, Max," he said now.

"You know what, Dooley? I think you're absolutely right. I mean, some individuals are born to be presidents and leaders of nations, while others, like us, are simply born to nap. And frankly I'm absolutely okay with that. It's a fate I'm completely at peace with."

"Me, too," Dooley said, and my eyes were already starting to drift closed.

"Hey, you guys!" suddenly a shrill voice sounded from the floor. I made the effort to shift my gaze to that particular spot and saw that Harriet and Brutus were among us once more.

"Hey, Harriet," I muttered. "What's up?" Not that I was dying to know, but even though my purpose in life may be to raise the art of napping to new and greater heights, that still leaves me with a basic respect for the niceties of social interaction.

"Guess what? I'm making my big debut tonight! Yay me!"

"Debut?" I asked. "Debut as what?"

"As a singer and stage presence. I just found out Gran is performing at the Hampton Cove Star tonight, and when I told her about my great ambition to be a singer, she invited me to perform one song as part of her act. She's been contracted to do two songs, and she's graciously offering me part of her allotted time for my debut. Isn't that just great?"

"Amazing," I said, not the least bit interested. "Wonderful. Fantastic. Knock 'em dead."

"Who is she going to knock dead?" asked Dooley.

"It's just an expression, Dooley," I said.

Harriet looked annoyed. "You don't have to be rude about it, Max," she said. "Just because you don't have any ambitions in life other than to lie on your flabby belly doesn't mean you should be demeaning to the rest of us, who have a higher calling."

"I'm not being demeaning," I said. "I said knock em dead, didn't I?"

"You're obviously saying I sing so bad people will drop dead. Well, let me tell you—"

"Knock em dead is a commonly used expression in showbiz, Harriet. It means that you'll do so well you'll knock the audience off their feet. You'll simply blow them away."

"Oh," she said, taken aback. "Well, thank you, Max. That's very nice of you to say."

"I'm doing backing vocals," Brutus muttered, looking pained. "And in front of some of the greats in showbiz, too." He smiled nervously. "Shouldn't we rehearse, though, smoochie poo?"

"No need," said Harriet decidedly. "Talent always shines through. Only talentless hacks rehearse. Real talent simply connects to the flow of divine genius and... dazzles." She did the jazz paws thing to show us what she meant.

"Connect to the flow of divine genius and dazzle," Brutus repeated, not looking entirely convinced. "Gotcha."

"You are coming, aren't you, Max? And you, Dooley" asked Harriet. "You have to see my debut. Or else you'll whine and complain about it for the rest of your napping lives."

"Sure," I said, and Harriet smiled, then stalked off, tail high and her head even higher.

"Maybe one rehearsal?" I could hear Brutus say as they walked out into the backyard.

"No means no, Brutus. We're stars. Stars don't rehearse. It might jinx us."

"No, no, of course," he said. "You're probably right." His tail was down, though, which is never a good sign.

"So is Harriet going to be a big star now, Max?" asked Dooley. "And Brutus?"

"I doubt it, Dooley. It takes talent to be a star, and Harriet, regardless of her numerous other and very wonderful qualities, lacks the one thing that makes a great singer."

"What is that?"

"She can't sing."

"Maybe people won't notice?"

"Oh, I think people will notice."

"So maybe you should tell her?"

"She wouldn't believe me if I did. In fact she'll probably get mad."

"But won't she make a fool of herself tonight?"

"If there's one thing I've learned in the course of my life, Dooley," I said, "it is that people can hardly tell the difference between a cat who can and a cat who can't sing. To humans it all sounds the same: like caterwauling. And they rarely enjoy it. And as far as other cats are concerned, I think we'll probably be the only cats present. The Mayor rarely invites felines to his shindigs and tonight won't be an exception I'm afraid."

"That's too bad, Max. After all we are members of his community."

"We're members of this community but we're not voters, Dooley. And we don't pay taxes. So as far as the Mayor is concerned we simply don't exist."

"If I were able to vote I'd vote for you, Max."

I laughed at this. "Max for mayor. Now wouldn't that be something?"

But Dooley was serious. "I think you'd make a great mayor, Max."

"Oh, Dooley. I'd make a terrible mayor. For one thing I can't even sign my own name, and it's hard to give an acceptance speech when no one in the audience understands what you're saying. No, trust me, buddy. No cat will ever be mayor of this town. That's one of those facts of life you better accept now or agonize about in silence forever."

"Well, fine. But I still think you'd be great."

"Thanks for the vote of confidence," I said with a smile. "I'll tell you one thing, though. If I were voted mayor I'd make you my second-in-command. And maybe we'd finally outlaw all dogs in this town. Make Hampton Cove the first dog-free town in America."

"See? Who wouldn't vote for that?"

"Dogs, maybe?"

He thought about this for a moment. "No, you're probably right. And if pets could vote, dogs would probably try to get a dog elected. And where would that leave us?"

"They'd probably turn Hampton Cove into the first cat-free town in America."

Dooley shook his head sadly. "We simply can't win, can we, Max?"

19

*O*delia arrived home wearing a deep frown. Writing the article, she'd realized how important it was to catch whoever had killed Chickie that morning, and she felt seriously hampered in her investigation by the Mayor's veto. She now had a strong suspicion Laron Weskit and the others might skip town tonight after the show, and there was nothing she could do about it. And the more she thought about that contingency the more upset she became. And as she paced her modest home, she suddenly caught sight of Max and Dooley, quietly dozing on the windowsill, and an idea struck her.

She approached her two cats and gently shook Max, then whispered in his ear, "Yoo-hoo, sleepyhead."

He made the cutest mewling sound, then opened his eyes and sleepily stared at her.

"I want you to go with me tonight to the Hampton Cove Star, Max. There's a big party and I want you to do some spying for me. Think you're up for it?"

Max yawned widely and said, "Is that the same party Harriet will sing at?"

"Harriet is going to sing tonight?"

"That's what she said. Gran is giving her a part of her slot."

Odelia frowned. "Gran is also going to sing?"

"It would appear so."

"Huh," said Odelia. "I didn't know that."

"Oh, yeah. It's going to be a family occasion."

"Well, so there you go. Another good reason to be my eyes and ears tonight."

"I want to come and see Harriet, too," said Dooley, stretching so much he almost dropped from the windowsill. She could just prevent him from toppling into the abyss.

"You can both come," she assured him. "You're not going to miss Harriet's show."

She thought for a moment. "So, um, I don't think cats are particularly welcome at this shindig. It's going to be very posh, with lots of celebrities and local politicians and businesspeople. The Mayor is going to give a speech, and hand the keys to the city to Charlie Dieber, but before that they reserved the stage for local talent—that's when Dad and Gran and Harriet will perform. And then at the end of the evening Charlie will sing a couple of songs, and a duet with Jamie. So what I need you to do is snoop around Laron's and Charlie's rooms. I'm not allowed to talk to them and neither is my uncle or Chase, but that isn't going to stop me from trying to find out as much about them as I can."

"We could watch the show from the wings," Max suggested. "And once Gran and Harriet's bits are done we could sneak out and go and search those rooms for you."

It sounded like a plan and she smiled. "You've got yourself a deal, buddy."

"So how are we going to get inside?" asked Max.

"Let me worry about that. Oh, and do you know where

Harriet and Brutus are? I want to ask them to join you. Four cats can snoop around a lot more than two."

"But Harriet will be on stage," said Dooley.

"I know, I mean when she's done performing."

And then she was off, in search of the other two members of her cat menagerie.

The Mayor might have prevented her from gaining access to four potential witnesses or even suspects, but he didn't know she had four furry secret weapons at her disposal.

She passed through the hedge that connected her backyard to her parents', and walked into the kitchen. Mom was preparing dinner, looking a little rattled.

"Have you seen Harriet and Brutus?" she asked. "I need to ask them something."

"Did you know your grandmother has decided to usurp your father?" asked Mom.

"Usurp Dad? What are you talking about?"

"Well, you remember how she said she wants to be the new Beyoncé?"

"How could I forget? Is this about Gran performing at tonight's event?"

"Your dad was supposed to be the local talent. But your gran has usurped him."

"I'm sure they'll both get to do a song. So have you seen Harriet and Brutus?"

"But that's just it. He's not going to do a song. Gran has taken his place. And I think this time she's gone too far. She knows how much your father was looking forward to tonight. First she took over his basement for her own rehearsals, and now she's taking over his gigs. Soon he will have to call it quits, and that would be a real shame."

"Why don't I talk to Gran?"

"Yes, please. Talk some sense into her. Make her realize

how much pain she's caused with this latest stunt. Tex is a good man, and all this nonsense is preying on his mind."

"I'll talk to her."

She moved into the living room, where Gran was watching *Jeopardy.*

"Have you seen Harriet and Brutus, Gran?" she asked.

"They're around somewhere," her grandmother grunted, her eyes fixed on the screen. "What is Belgium!"

"Around where? I've been looking all over the place."

"Aren't they over at yours? They usually hang around your place around this time. Harriet figures this house is too noisy, and she's taken a sudden dislike to *Jeopardy* for some reason. No idea why. Best show on TV. Who is Cary Grant!"

Odelia took a seat next to her grandmother. "Gran, I need to talk to you."

"Uh-oh."

"Yeah. Is it true you took over Dad's gig at tonight's event?"

"I did no such thing. Can I help it if the Mayor thinks my act is better suited for an event of this magnitude than your dad's?"

"Did you ask him to bump Dad from the lineup?"

"No, I didn't. All I did was call Marjorie, who's in charge of the thing, and ask her what she preferred: three boring old coots singing a boring old jazz song, or a fun new act fronted by an exciting hit sensation. A no-brainer. She practically jumped at the chance."

"But Gran—you know how much Dad was looking forward to tonight. He and the other doctors have been practicing all week. It was supposed to be his crowning glory."

"Look, darling, it's show business, not show charity. You have to be tough to make it in this business, and I'm sorry to say that Tex just ain't got what it takes."

"That's very mean-spirited of you, Gran. I didn't know you hated Dad so much."

Gran looked up with a frown. "I don't hate your father. In fact I kinda like him. In his own goofy way he's good for Marge, and he's a good dad. But this is my chance to shine, honey, and it may very well be my last one, too. I'm seventy-five. I might never get to perform in front of this crowd again. This is my shot at the big leagues and I owe it to myself to grab it. For Tex this is just a fun little hobby. For me it's make-or-break time."

Odelia shook her head. "Still, it's a pretty raw deal for Dad."

"Okay, fine, you're probably right. You know what I'll do? I'll give one of my two slots to Tex. How about that? I'll go first, and Tex can go next. That all right with you?"

"I thought you gave one of your two slots to Harriet?"

"They can do the interlude."

Odelia smiled and got up. "Thanks, Gran. I'll tell Dad right now. He'll be thrilled."

"And don't accuse me of never doing anything for this family!" Gran cried as Odelia left the room. "I'm only making this sacrifice because I care!"

"Thanks!" she yelled, and hurried into the kitchen to tell her mother the good news.

20

That evening, the Poole family was out in full force. Gran and her band were due to perform, and so were Tex and his Singing Doctors. As a reporter for the *Hampton Cove Gazette*, Odelia had snagged a much-coveted invitation, and as a plus-one to the talent, Marge was also there.

Odelia had managed to smuggle Dooley and me in via the hotel's service entrance. No cats or other pets were allowed, not even the pets the stars usually lugged around, like Chihuahuas or pugs or even those potbellied pigs. The only exception to the rule were pets as part of the evening's entertainment, like Harriet and Brutus, who were now holed up in Gran and Tex's dressing room. And with them present, Odelia wisely figured we wouldn't look out of place either. So she'd dropped us off around the corner from the Hampton Cove Star, we'd quickly made our way to the service entrance, and had waited patiently for Odelia to usher us in. Right on schedule the door had opened and Odelia had bundled us both up in her arms and quickly deposited us in Gran's care.

I was surprised to find that Harriet was now as nervous as Brutus was. "I can't do this!" she cried, pacing the room. "People are going to laugh at me! They're going to think this is all a big joke! Oh, Gran, why did you ever agree to this! Why, oh, why!"

Tex was also pacing the room, and didn't look very relaxed either, nor did the two doctors who were part of his band. Denby Jennsen is a man who could have played a part in *Grey's Anatomy*, he's that movie-star handsome, and Cary Horsfield is as distinguished-looking as Tex. All three were dressed in matching charcoal suits.

Meanwhile, Gran was entertaining her own band, which consisted of half a dozen elderly men, all dressed in white tuxedos. Gran herself looked like a million bucks. Her face was made up, her hair done up, and... she was only wearing white underwear. Lacy bra, lacy panties, silk stockings and even a garter belt. She also wore red stilettos.

"You can do this, twinkle toes," said Brutus, affectionately patting Harriet's paw.

"They'll think we're a pair of freaks! No cats have ever performed live in front of an audience like this, except to jump through hoops or dangle from a trapeze. Why did I ever think this was a good idea?" She directed a dark look at her mate. "Why didn't you talk me out of this, Brutus. Why?!"

Dooley and I watched the scene with keen interest. It's a lot more fun to be in the dressing room before the big show when you're not an actual part of the lineup.

"I think Harriet will do great," I said. "Usually when singers are this nervous it's because they're about to blow everyone away."

"Or she will be so bad she can already feel it," Dooley said.

"That's also a possibility," I allowed.

Whatever the case, a bomb or a hit, the show was bound

to be a smash. The local doctor, his elderly mother-in-law and their cats? What more could an audience want?

We walked out of the dressing room into the corridor and padded towards the stage. Watching on from the wings, I saw that the ballroom was gradually filling up. I could see the Mayor and his wife, and I could see Dan Goory, Odelia's editor, who was also a guest. He was there along with his wife, who looked resplendent in a shimmering evening gown. In fact I saw pretty much everyone who was someone in Hampton Cove, as well as plenty of the town's nobodies. I also recognized Laron Weskit and his wife, whose pictures Odelia had shown us. They were seated at the Mayor's table —guests of honor.

If we'd wanted to, we could have snuck up to their room right then. But we'd already decided to wait and see the show first. It wasn't something I was prepared to miss.

And yet for a moment it looked as if that was exactly what was going to happen, when a man dressed like a bellhop grabbed us both by the necks and growled angrily, "How did you two hairy pests get in here?" and started dragging us away!

Lucky for us Odelia was also keeping an eye on the proceedings, and quickly negotiated our release. She then bent down, and placed a nice ribbon around my neck, a small card dangling from it, and repeated the procedure on Dooley.

"There," she said. "Now no one can accuse you of being interlopers. This makes it clear you're part of the evening's entertainment. Oh, and those badges will also grant you access to certain rooms," she added with a wink. "Don't lose them, you guys."

"We sure won't," I said, happy we were in the clear.

And then it was time for the show to begin. The lights in

the ballroom were dimmed, and with stragglers still filing in, the curtains swung open, and Tex appeared on stage.

"Look, it's Tex!" Dooley whispered excitedly.

"I know!" I whispered back, equally excited.

Next thing we knew, the band launched into a jazzy rendition of *My Bonnie Lies over the Ocean*, Denby crooning, Tex slapping a drum kit, and Cary plucking at a guitar.

They didn't even sound half bad. Dr. Denby, apart from looking like George Clooney in his *ER* heyday, has one of those rich, deep baritones, and a smile that lights up a room. He did so now, and at the end of the song women clapped excitedly, the husbands less so.

"That wasn't so bad," said Dooley as he put his paws together.

"Not bad at all," I agreed, following suit. It's a pity our paws are outfitted with soft pink pads. It hampers our ability to applaud, but we still gave it our best shot for Tex.

Next up were Gran and her six Dapper Dans. She'd draped herself across a piano for some reason, and huskily began to sing *Like a Virgin*. She sounded as if she had a frog in her throat, but maybe that was the style she was going for. The only role the men played was to sing backing vocals (*like a vi-i-i-ir-gin*) and from time to time lift her off the piano and then to put her back. There was also music playing, probably produced by a tape.

"What is she doing?" asked Dooley after a while.

"I have no idea," I said.

"And why is she dressed in her underwear?"

"Maybe she forgot to bring her clothes?"

When we'd seen her backstage in her underwear, I'd figured she would put on her dress at the last minute, but now it turned out this was it—this was her stage costume.

The men now placed her back on top of the piano, where she began writhing about, trying to look sexy. Then the men picked her up again and deposited her on the floor, where she proceeded to teeter from the left side of the stage to the right on her high heels, all the while moaning her way through the song, the men darting around her.

"I think it's supposed to be sexy," I finally said.

The men had picked Gran up again and tried to heave her onto the piano. Clearly they were all starting to feel the strain, for they ended up dropping her to the floor. So Gran decided to remain where she was while throatily pushing out those final few notes.

There wasn't even a hint of applause this time. A lot of stunned people sat staring, waiters had stopped waiting, and smartphones were out, filming the weird spectacle.

And they'd seen nothing yet, for as Gran got up and cleared the stage, Harriet and Brutus walked on. Harriet took a slight bow and, much to the consternation of those present, started yowling. I think she was going for *Like a Prayer*, in line with Gran's performance, but unfortunately stress must have affected her vocal cords, for all that came out were a series of disjointed notes. Brutus, meanwhile, tried to act like a beatbox, but messed up when he ended up blowing a series of extended raspberries instead.

"I don't recognize this song," said Dooley.

"I think it's Madonna's *Like a Prayer*," I said.

"Oh, right," said Dooley.

We both winced as Harriet launched into the chorus, and people started pressing their hands against their ears. Never a good sign for a debut artist's first live show.

She must have realized things weren't going well, for suddenly she broke off prematurely, and hurriedly left the stage, Brutus still blowing raspberries, as if he'd forgotten where his off-switch was located. Finally he realized he was alone on stage, grinned nervously, and skipped into the wings like a foal on its first foray into the field.

For a moment, all was silent, but then the room plunged into confused talk and chattering. The Mayor looked embarrassed, and the Weskits sat stony-faced. They'd probably anticipated something dignified. With standing. Something along the lines of the *American Music Awards* or the *Grammy's*. They got *America's Got Talent* instead.

21

*B*ehind us, Odelia had materialized. Whether she was shocked or enchanted by the performance of her grandmother and Harriet was impossible to deduce from her expression. She had a sparkle in her eye, though. The sparkle of a reporter who's just picked up the scent of a great story. To us she merely whispered, "Go, go, go!"

And so go we went.

Odelia had opened a door that led to the hotel's backstairs and we quickly made our way up until we'd reached the fourth floor. I took a moment to catch my breath, and to our elation we found the door easily yielding to pressure and the hallway empty.

"This is going well, Dooley," I commented as I looked up and down the hallway. "I don't think anyone saw us."

"But what about Harriet and Brutus?" he asked. "Weren't they supposed to join us?"

"I think they're probably still recovering from their performance."

"They didn't do very well, did they, Max?"

"No, I think it's safe to say that they didn't."

"Probably nerves."

"'Yeah, it's a different thing to sing in front of cats than a room full of humans."

We were traipsing along the hallway, looking left and right as we went, and making sure we weren't caught. The hallway was easily as nice as the ballroom. Gilded sconces along the walls, gorgeous velvety wallpaper, that nice thick red carpet. Everything for the hotel's VIP guests. Dooley was announcing the room numbers out loud, both proving he could count and making sure we didn't skip past our destination, and finally we'd reached the Weskits' room. I glanced up at the door handle, which was way higher than I'd anticipated, and sighed.

"I don't know about you, Dooley, but I can't possibly jump that high."

"Do you want me to give it a try?" And without waiting for my response, he performed a nice standing high jump. He reached about halfway to the handle, which was outfitted with one of those panels you hold your badge against for easy access.

"Close but no cigar," I told him encouragingly.

"That's all right," he said. "I don't smoke." He made a second attempt, but reached even less high than before. Cats are great jumpers, but we're not rabbits or kangaroos.

I listened carefully for that telltale clicking sound that indicates the badge has done what it's supposed to do but no luck so far. No clicking sound and no access for us.

"Can't you hover in the air a little longer?" I asked. "I think the little gizmo needs time to figure out a badge is near. And try to hold up the badge. Hold it as high as you can."

So Dooley kept on jumping, trying to hold up the badge with his paws. If the selection committee for the Olympic Games had seen him, they'd definitely have given him points for effort. Unfortunately even cats as fit and healthy as Dooley reach the end of their tether, and as Dooley sat on the floor, panting heavily, the door was still as closed as ever.

And as Dooley got some air into his lungs, I spotted a cart at the end of the hallway. It was one of those carts used by room service people, and I could spot a couple of empty glasses on top of it, as well as a bucket with a champagne bottle peeping out at the top. "Maybe we could roll that cart over here and jump on top of it?" I now suggested.

"Good… (pant pant) idea… (pant pant) Max. Let's… (pant pant) give… (pant pant) it… (pant pant) a shot (closing pant)."

So we gamboled along the corridor—that is to say, I gamboled and Dooley dragged his weary body along as fast as he could—and when we reached the cart I saw that, indeed, it was equipped with nifty little wheels. So we both pushed, and soon the cart was rolling along nicely at a brisk pace. Unfortunately I think we must have put a little too much push into the thing, or maybe the carpet wasn't as thick and plush as I'd anticipated, for we overshot the room and still the cart kept on zipping along. It proceeded to pick up speed, until it slammed against the wall at the end. For a moment, bucket and glasses waggled precariously, then, like lemmings, collectively made the jump. The first glass was fine, but when the second one fell on top of it, it gave up the fight and broke, and so did the third, and the fourth, and when the bucket tipped over and dropped down on top of all of them, it crushed what remained of the glassware.

"I'm not going near that," announced Dooley.

This may be a good time to remind you that cats do not wear shoes. So we try to steer clear of sharp objects on the floor, be they glass or other items that cut our tender paws.

To my elation I immediately spotted a second cart. So we decided to repeat the procedure, only this time Dooley pushed and I walked in front of the cart to provide a measure of stoppage. We managed to maneuver the cart where it needed to be. Dooley made one final jump, and landed squarely on top of the cart, held out his badge, and there was that delicious, much-sought-after clicking sound: open Sesame!

Once inside, we quickly spread out. I headed into the kitchen, hoping the Weskits had pets and had left the pet food out, and Dooley moved into the bedroom for a brief nap.

I quickly discovered that the Weskits did not have pets, and the only food I could find in the kitchen was leftover pizza. I'm not choosy when I'm hungry, though, so I took a tentative bite. And as I digested this first nibble, I decided the pizza was fit for feline consumption and quickly devoured a large slice, leaving a smaller slice for Dooley. Feeling fortified, I went in search of that all-telling clue that Odelia had mentioned. She had no idea what it might look like, but had assured us that if we found it, we'd recognize it for what it was: The One Clue That Rules All Other Clues (or TOCTRAOC).

And I'd just wended my way in the general direction of the bedroom to see what Dooley was up to, when I was startled to come across two large eyes glowing in the dark, staring back at me. I immediately recognized them as belonging to the Felis catus species.

In other words, the Weskits did have a pet, and that pet was a cat.

---

*O*delia, along with her mom, Uncle Alec and Chase, sat one table removed from the Mayor's table, so she was able to keep a close eye on the Weskits, Laron and Shannon. So far the couple hadn't moved from their seats, so Max and Dooley were in the clear.

"That was terrible," said her mother as she distractedly picked from a cheese platter.

"I thought Dad was pretty good. Not exactly his crowd, but still a solid performance."

"Your dad was fantastic, but your grandmother!" Marge shook her head. "What was she thinking!"

Odelia grinned. "It was a little weird. She was probably thinking she was fifty years younger."

"I should have stayed for rehearsals. I would never have allowed her on stage dressed like that."

"To be fair, Marge," said Uncle Alec as he swirled the remnants of a nice burgundy in his glass, "even if you'd told her not to perform she'd gone ahead and done it anyway."

"I know, Alec—she never listens to anyone, that's the

problem. And that poor Harriet and Brutus. What an awful, humiliating spectacle. Where are they, anyway?"

Odelia leaned in and whispered into her mom's ear, "They're upstairs, checking out Charlie and Jamie's room, while Max and Dooley are going through the Weskits' stuff."

"Well, I hope they find something."

"And I hope they don't get caught," said Chase, who looked worried.

"They won't get caught, and even if they are, hotel staff will simply throw them out."

"What are you hoping they'll find?" asked Uncle Alec, accepting a refill from a waiter.

"Anything, something. I don't know. It's frustrating not being able to interview them."

"Tomorrow," said the Chief. "Tomorrow we can interview them all we want."

"And do you seriously expect them to stick around for us to do that? I'll bet their flights are booked and they'll be gone at first light."

"Possibly, but that would simply make them more suspect. And wherever they go, there's police there, too, and a simple request from me will see them interrogated."

"Still, I feel more relaxed knowing our cats are going through their things with a fine-tooth comb."

"Or a fine-claw paw," Chase quipped.

Just then, Gran joined them at their table, accompanied by Tex. A scarlet blush mantled Gran's cheeks, but at least she'd covered up her Madonna-style lingerie.

"And?" Gran asked as she took a seat. "What did you think of the show?"

Chase murmured something noncommittal, while Uncle Alec stared at the ceiling.

"It was terrible!" Marge cried, unable to restrain herself.

"What the hell were you thinking? You turned us into the town's laughingstock! How am I ever going to face people now? And have you considered Alec's reputation? Or Tex's? Or Odelia's?"

The corners of Gran's lips dropped. "Is that a way to encourage the only star in your family? I'll have you know I got a lot of compliments backstage. Charlie Dieber knocked on my dressing room door and personally told me how rad he thought I was."

"He was watching?" asked Odelia.

"Of course. Charlie, Jamie, they both watched from the wings. And now that I've got some buzz going, I just know I'll be able to take this thing into the stratosphere."

"Do you honestly think your performance was good?" asked Marge. "You sang completely out of tune, you looked like a hoary harlot, and those men! They should be ashamed of themselves, the way they behaved—salivating over you like… like… johns!"

"That's the difference between a star and a nobody like you, Marge," Gran snapped. "A star is out there, shining brightly, while ordinary people like you only excel at petty jealousy. Now if you'll excuse me, I'm going to mingle and stoke up some more buzz."

"Mingle!" Marge cried as Gran walked away. "You should apologize to the Mayor!"

"Oh, just leave her be," said Alec. "I think it's nice she has a hobby. Keeps her out of trouble."

"God," said Marge, and plunked her head against the table, upsetting the tableware.

"Oh, honey," said Tex, rubbing her between the shoulder blades. "It's gonna be fine."

Marge lifted her head. "Do you really believe what she said about Charlie Dieber complimenting her on being 'rad?'"

"Yeah, that actually happened. I was right there when he told her."

"The world has gone stark-raving mad," Marge groaned, and thunked her head again.

❧

"*L*et's go, let's go, let's go!" said Jerry as Johnny closed the door of the car. They darted across the road and immediately disappeared into the alley next to the hotel.

"Do you think this bag is big enough, Jer?" asked Johnny, showing Jerry a ginormous gym bag.

"I like it when you think big, Johnny," said Jerry with a grin.

"I hope they've got Rolexes," said Johnny, sounding like a kid on Christmas morning. "If they got some nice Rolexes I might grab one for me. I've always liked Rolexes."

"Once we pull this off, you can have all the Rolexes in the world," said Jerry, who was also in buoyant mood. It was the adrenaline, and the excitement of a job well-planned and about to be well-executed. He never got tired of that zippy sensation.

"I just hope there's no security," said Johnny, returning to his favorite theme.

"I told you a million times already, Johnny. All the body-guards will be downstairs with the people they're supposed to be guarding with their bodies, not upstairs."

"And I hope they didn't use the hotel safe. I hate it when they do that. So unfair. But even if they did, I'm going to crack that safe, Jer. I'm gonna crack it open like a coconut."

"That's the spirit, Johnny," said Jerry. "That's that will to win right there."

They'd arrived at the fire escape and now climbed the

metal stairs to the fourth floor, where the rooms of the Weskits and that twerp pop singer and his girl were located.

"First the Weskits," Jerry said.

"And then the twerp," Johnny cheerfully sang.

It took Johnny only a couple of seconds of fiddling with the lock to open the fire exit door and then they were in. They jogged along the corridor in search of the Weskits' room and once they'd found it, it was only a few moments before that lock too, yielded to the power of Johnny's toolkit and experience. They quickly burst in and closed the door.

"Let's do this!" Jerry whispered.

"Hallelujah!" Johnny yodeled.

"*T*respassers," said the eyes that glowed in the dark. Or at least the creature to whom the eyes belonged. As a rule, eyes rarely burst into speech.

"No, visitors," I corrected the feline. "Friendly visitors that come in peace."

The cat was silent for a brief moment, then finally emerged from the shadows so I could see it whole. It was one of those hairless cats—the ones without any fur—and for a moment I couldn't help but stare at it. Next to me, Dooley had also materialized, attracted by the voices, and was gripped by the same sudden fascination with this rare creature, for the cat grunted, "Cat got your tongue? Never seen a hairless cat before?"

"Um, as a matter of fact I haven't," I confessed. "This is a first for me."

"Oh, you poor cat," said Dooley, perhaps not striking the right tone. "Did it hurt?"

"Did what hurt?" the cat growled, its eyes narrowing dangerously.

"When they shaved you. It must have hurt. What did they

use? A razor blade or an electric razor? And who did it? Your humans or a professional? A professional, probably. At one of those pet salons. I don't see any shaving nicks. When Chase shaves in the morning he always manages to cut himself. Odelia's told him several times he should use an electric razor but he insists they don't produce the same smooth finish as his trusty Gillette. To each their own, I guess, though I think Odelia's right, to be honest—you're probably wondering who Odelia is. She's our human, and she would never, ever shave us. Except if we asked her, of course, which we never will. Which isn't to say I don't approve of your personal life choice, sir or ma'am. Like I said, to each their own."

The cat was producing a low growling sound at the back of its throat, and I quickly nudged Dooley in the ribs. "You're blabbing, Dooley. Maybe now is a good time to zip it." I understood where he was coming from, of course. Seeing your first hairless cat in the flesh, so to speak, tends to produce a bit of a shock. That certainly was my experience.

"First of all, nobody shaves me," said the cat now. "Secondly, this is what I've always looked like. I don't have the advantage of fur, which is why I would prefer it if you didn't make any cracks about it. Now back to my question: why are you trespassing?"

"Like I said, we're not trespassing," I said. "Well, technically perhaps we are, but it's for a good cause. You see, a, um, good friend of our humans died this morning—she was murdered, in fact—and now we're trying to figure out who could have done that to her."

Dooley was still eyeing the cat with undiminished fascination. "Can I…" He approached the cat. "Can I touch it?"

"*It?* I'm a person, not a thing," said the cat icily.

"I know, but I've never seen a cat like you. What's your name? Are you a he or a she?"

"My name is Cleo," said the cat, giving Dooley a nasty look, "and I'm a female, can't you tell?"

"Well, no, actually I can't," said Dooley. "You look like no cat I've ever seen. Does she look like any cat you've ever seen, Max?"

"Look, it doesn't matter, Dooley," I said, "and frankly I think you're getting on Cleo's nerves, so let's just tone it down a little, shall we?"

"No, I like his candor," said Cleo. "Most cats I meet act very snootily, figuring they need to make a big impression on me or something. So I find your honesty refreshing, cat. What are your names, by the way?"

"Dooley," said Dooley, "and this is my best friend Max."

"Well, nice to make your acquaintance, Dooley and Max," said Cleo, losing some of her earlier frostiness. "So this person who got killed, what's their name?"

"Chickie Hay," I said. "We're trying to find out who killed her and why."

"Chickie is dead? Oh, that's such a pity. My humans really liked her, and so did those next door."

"Charlie Dieber and Jamie Borowiak," I said, nodding.

"Wait, I thought your humans hated Chickie Hay?" said Dooley.

"Yeah, that's the information we got," I said.

"Not true. There was bad blood between them, sure, but that was all business related. As a person they liked her and admired her for the career she built. I liked her, too. Nice songs. Though to be honest I'm more of a jazz cat myself."

"Then you'll like our human's dad," said Dooley. "He's a musician and he plays jazz."

"What kind of jazz?" asked Cleo, her interest piqued.

"Um…" I stared at Dooley and Dooley stared at me. "No idea, actually," I said.

"Big band, bebop, contemporary, free jazz, ragtime, Latin jazz?"

"Is that all… music?" asked Dooley.

"Types of jazz music, yeah."

"How come you know so much about this stuff?" I asked.

"That's what you get when you live with a true music fan," said Cleo with a deferential little smile.

"Laron likes jazz?" I asked.

"Loves jazz. He plays a little jazz himself. So what kind of music are you guys into?"

But unfortunately—or fortunately—our musical preference would remain a secret to Cleo, for the door to the room had suddenly opened and two men walked in. One was big and burly and the other thin and scrawny and as they stood illuminated against the backdrop of the hallway lights, I thought for a moment I'd seen them both before.

"Hey, I think I've seen these guys before," Dooley said, confirming my suspicions.

Then again, in our line of work you meet so many people it's hard to keep track.

"More intruders," said Cleo with a sad shake of the head.

"Maybe they're visitors, like us," said Dooley as he watched the men close the door and enter the room. They were both carrying big empty gym bags.

"Doubtful," said Cleo. "They look like a bunch of crooks to me, and trust me, I know the difference. If humans are as rich as mine, a lot of people want to share in that wealth, usually without asking permission first."

"I'll look in here," said the skinny one. "You try the bedroom. And focus on high-value items only, Johnny. I'll bet these rich bozos got plenty of gold and jewels lying around."

"Isn't that rappers, though, Jer?" asked the one named Johnny. "Rappers like gold."

"Rappers, pop stars, who cares? They all love jewels and so do we."

"Gotcha, Jer," said Johnny, and started rifling through one of the cabinets.

"Looks like you're right, Cleo," I said. "I think these men are here to steal from your human."

"Of course I'm right."

"So what do we do now? We probably shouldn't let this happen, right?"

"No, we shouldn't. Lucky for us the hotel has taken precautions for this type of contingency." And with a deft trot she stalked over to the door, and placed her paw against what looked like a small metal plate. Moments later a deadbolt was shoved home in the door, something clattered down in front of the windows, and the room was suddenly flooded with pulsating red light, accompanied by a loud wailing siren.

The crook named Jerry cursed loudly and started pulling at the door, which wouldn't budge, then ran over to a connecting door, which offered the same resistance, and finally tried the window, only to discover that a steel shutter had slammed down to seal it off. There was no escape. He then resorted to pulling at his own hair. "Not again!" he cried.

"I think we're busted, Jer," said Johnny, stomping in from the bedroom.

"I *know* we're busted, you idiot! Someone must have tripped the alarm!"

"You didn't tell me about no alarm, Jer."

"That's because nobody told *me* about no danged alarm!"

"So what do we do now, Jerry?"

"Now we wait for the cops to show up."

"But I don't want to wait for the cops to show up, Jerry! The cops will arrest us, and I don't want to be arrested."

"Stay calm, Johnny!" yelled Jerry, not exactly the epitome of tranquility himself. "And when they arrive simply follow my lead. Tell 'em you thought this was our room."

"Maybe we should tell 'em the truth."

"No, Johnny. *Don't you dare.* Repeat after me: I thought this was my room."

"Do you think they'll believe us?"

"Of course they'll believe us! We just have to stick to our story, no matter what."

Johnny was sweating profusely now. "I'm a lousy liar, Jer. You know I am."

"Don't you dare tell them the truth, Johnny. Just do as I say and we'll be all right."

"Okay, Jer. We show them the key and tell 'em we accidentally got the wrong room."

"Don't show them the key!"

"Why not?"

"Because then they'll know we got an accomplice!"

"You mean the same accomplice who forgot to mention the alarm?"

"Just stick to the story and we'll be okay."

"I don't know, Jer."

"Stick to the story!"

"They don't appear to be the smartest crooks in the business," said Cleo.

"Max! I think I know these guys," suddenly said Dooley. "Aren't they the same ones who tried to rob Odelia? And then you and me told Chase and Chase arrested them?"

"Hey, I think you're right, Dooley."

Moments later, the alarm stopped whining, and the door opened. The first one to burst through was Chase, quickly followed by Uncle Alec. Chase was holding up a gun. "Hands behind your heads! On your knees!" he yelled, and Johnny and Jerry promptly did as they were told.

"I thought this was my room!" Johnny cried, eyes wide as he took in that big gun and the even bigger cop handling it.

"We must have gotten the floors mixed," Jerry said, producing a strained smile.

"Well, well, well. If it ain't Johnny Carew and Jerry Vale. So we meet again."

"Hi, Detective Kingsley," said Johnny sheepishly. "You're not going to arrest us, are you? I really thought this was our room," he added like a well-trained parrot.

"So where's your key?" asked Uncle Alec.

Johnny produced his key card, drawing a low hissing sound from his partner in crime. Uncle Alec took the card and studied it. "So who's your accomplice?"

Jerry and Johnny shared a look. "I don't know what you're talking about, Chief," said Jerry. "We're guests at this hotel and we thought this was our room. Can we help it if all these rooms look the same?" He laughed, but it sounded more like a horse neighing.

"Yeah, can we help it if all the rooms in this hotel look the same?" asked Johnny, actually perking up now that he figured their ruse was working.

"This is a very special key card," said Uncle Alec, waving the card. "It's called a master key. It allows access to all the rooms in the building. Only hotel personnel carry these. So how did you get hold of it?"

"Receptionist must have made a mistake," said Jerry with a shrug.

"Yeah, the receptionist gave us this key," said Johnny, lifting his massive shoulders.

"Why are you both dressed in black, with rubber-soled shoes and rubber gloves?" asked Chase.

"We like to dress in black," said Jerry. "And we're both germophobic."

"Yeah, we don't like Germans," said Johnny with a quick glance at Jerry.

Uncle Alec had crouched down next to the gym bags and was rummaging through them. He brought out a flashlight, a drill, a hammer, a chisel, a Swiss knife, and a box full of weird-looking metal instruments. "And I'll bet this is your luggage," he said grimly.

"We're like the Boy Scouts of America," Jerry declared solemnly. "Always prepared."

"Yeah, we take that stuff everywhere we go," said Johnny. "You never know when you might need a hammer, or a pair of pliers."

"Look, I'll make you a deal," said Uncle Alec, getting up. "If you give us the name of your accomplice I'll talk to the judge. Tell him you cooperated like two nice crooks. If not, I'll throw the book at you, and you're looking at extended jail time. So what do you say?"

Jerry was already shaking his head, but Johnny's eyebrows had shot up and he had a mournful expression on his face. It was the expression of a man about to spill his guts.

"No, Johnny," said Jerry, who'd noticed the same thing. "Don't you do it."

"But, Jerry. I don't want to go back to prison."

"No. Don't you do it, Johnny. Don't you dare."

"His name is Camillo Equius," Johnny suddenly blurted out. "He told us Laron Weskit and his wife were staying here tonight, and that Dieber kid, and he gave us the key."

"Thanks, Johnny. You know the drill," Uncle Alec said as he unclipped a pair of handcuffs from his belt. "You're both under arrest. Anything you say—"

"Johnny, you idiot!" said Jerry. "I told you to keep your big mouth shut!"

"I'm sorry, Jer. But he made us a deal I couldn't refuse!"

"I'm never working with you again. You hear me! This partnership is over!"

"It's all for the best, Jer," said Johnny as both men were led out by Chase. "The Chief is a good man. He'll keep up his end of the bargain. I know he will. Isn't that right, Chief?"

"Never! I'm never working with you again! Never, never, never!"

Laron Weskit and his wife, who apparently had been waiting right outside, now entered the room. "So?" said Laron. "What did they take?"

"Nothing," said Uncle Alec. "We got here just in time."

"I don't get it," said Laron, planting his hands on his hips. "I didn't switch on the alarm, because Cleo is here and she might accidentally trip it."

"I think Cleo is the one who tripped it, sir," said Alec, gesturing to the hairless cat.

Laron's eyebrows shot up. "My cat tripped the alarm? That's impossible."

"You'd be surprised how clever cats can be, sir," said Uncle Alec as he gave me and Dooley a wink.

I tried to wink back but found it a little hard. It's one of those things you have to practice first.

Shannon Weskit bent over and picked Cleo up in her arms. "Did you save us, Cleo, darling? Did you? You're a regular hero, aren't you? You're a real wonder cat."

"I don't believe it," said Laron, shaking his head. "There has to be some other explanation. Cats don't trigger alarms. That's dogs."

"Cats are smart," said his wife, who obviously was more of a cat person than her husband.

"Yeah, yeah, yeah," said Laron, and started doing the rounds of the suite to see for himself if nothing had been taken.

Just then, the connecting door flew open and Charlie

Dieber and Jamie burst in. "Did they take anything?" asked Charlie anxiously.

"Not that I can see," said Laron.

"Cleo sounded the alarm," said Shannon. "Isn't she a clever little puss? Yes, you are, Cleo. Yes, you are."

"So weird," said Charlie, who looked like a teenager, but a teenager with tattoos running up and down his arms. "There's two cats in our room that weren't there before. And I have no idea how they got there."

And as if to lend credence to his words, Harriet and Brutus walked in!

"Hey, isn't that the cats that sang at the show?" asked Jamie, a petite young woman with long dark hair and a serious look on her face.

"They sure look like them," said Laron.

"But how did they get into our room?" asked Charlie.

"Maybe they're with the burglars," said Jamie.

Just then, Laron's eyes fell on Dooley and me. "Well, I'll be damned," he said as he scratched his head. "Look. More cats. Where did they come from?"

Oops. Busted!

A family meeting had been called and we were part of the agenda.

"Odelia doesn't look happy," said Dooley.

"No, she doesn't look happy at all," Brutus agreed.

We were in the living room of Marge and Tex's home, and all the humans had gathered for this occasion: Uncle Alec was there, and Chase, and Odelia, of course, and Marge and Tex and Gran. The feline members of the family had been relegated to the floor, where we now sat like four defendants about to be subjected to cross-examination.

"Maybe we need to ask for a lawyer," said Dooley.

He was right, and I was already looking around for the Bible on which we'd soon have to swear to tell the truth and nothing but the truth.

"We didn't even have time to go through that room," said Harriet. "The moment we got in, this loud alarm started blaring, and soon after, Charlie and Jamie burst in."

"How did you get into their room?" I asked.

"Odelia had given us key cards," said Brutus.

"Same thing here," I said. "Very clever, too."

"Very clever, if only those crooks hadn't chosen that exact moment to break in."

"Okay, let's begin," said Uncle Alec. "First off, Johnny Carew and Jerry Vale are back where they belong: in jail. Johnny cracked first, and confessed. We also arrested Camillo Aquius, one of the receptionists and apparently in cahoots with the crooks, in exchange for a percentage of the loot, who provided them with information and a master key."

"What they hadn't counted on was the presence of Cleo," said Chase. "Who managed to sound the alarm, and make sure a happy ending was had by all."

Except Johnny and Jerry, obviously.

"Speaking of happy endings, did you guys manage to find out anything?" asked Odelia. She'd directed these words at us, and they were definitely better than 'Do you have anything to say for yourselves?'

I cleared my throat. "According to Cleo, Laron and his wife respected Chickie a lot, and thought she was an amazing and talented person. They had some business disagreements but that wasn't all that important, at least according to her. All in all, she gave me the impression that Laron would never harm a hair on Chickie's head."

"What is he saying?" asked Chase with a smile.

Odelia quickly translated my words for the non-feline speakers in the room, and Uncle Alec nodded. "It doesn't mean much, but at least it says something about motive."

"So where are we on the investigation?" asked Odelia, directing a quizzical look at her uncle and boyfriend.

"Nowhere, that's where we are," said Uncle Alec.

"Plenty of suspects but nothing conclusive," Chase agreed.

"So we need to keep digging," said Odelia. "We need to keep talking to people, asking all the right questions."

"I talked to the Mayor at the party tonight," said Uncle

Alec, "and he said that if we don't crack this case soon, he'll be compelled to bring in the state police."

"Who'll take over the investigation and sink our reputations," Chase said somberly.

"State police or not, I'm not going to stop digging until I find something," said Odelia.

All eyes suddenly turned to us, and Brutus muttered, "This is it. Get ready for a kicking, you guys."

But instead of a kicking, Odelia gave us a heartfelt smile. "I think it's fair to say that the only ones who've managed to get anywhere in this case are Max, Dooley, Brutus and Harriet. You've figured out the best clues, and you've talked to the only witnesses who were actually able to tell you something. In fact I would love to suggest to the Mayor not to call in the state police but to deputize the four of you instead."

Marge laughed. "I'd love to be there when you have that conversation."

"Yeah, me too," said Uncle Alec, who didn't seem overly excited at the prospect of welcoming four cats into his squad.

"I'm just kidding, of course," said Odelia, "though not about your achievements. So I would like to thank you, and I would like to tell you to keep up the good work." And then she turned to her grandmother. "And now for the real reason we are all gathered here. Gran, I think it's time you and Dad buried the hatchet. You've been at each other's throats for too long and it's starting to affect the way the community views this family."

"They think we're all nuts," said Marge. "We're the laughingstock of this town."

"I think that's an excellent suggestion," said Gran. "And I'm very happy that you've finally decided to apologize, Tex." A set look had come over her face. "Well? I'm waiting."

"I, um…" said Tex.

"It isn't Tex who should apologize," said Marge. "First you walk out on him and leave him to deal with his patients all by himself, then you fail to live up to your promise to support his new band. And to add insult to injury you made fools of us all by gyrating across the stage dressed in your underwear and looking like an idiot. So I think you owe us all an apology. Not just Tex. Your whole family. We're all affected by your nonsense."

Harsh words, but maybe Gran deserved them. She clearly hadn't expected it, though, for her face displayed a distinctly mutinous look. "Are you nuts? I'm the only one in this family who's trying to build a career. To make something of themselves. I'm doing you proud. So you should be thanking me, instead of criticizing me."

"Your performance was terrible, Ma," said Uncle Alec. "Crawling over that stage in that outfit, with those old fools drooling all over you. I think I speak for all of us when I tell you that you crossed a line tonight. A line that should never have been crossed."

"I crossed a line? Well, if that's how you feel," said Gran, pressing her lips together. "I'll have you know that I talked to Laron after the show, and he offered me a contract."

They all stared at the old lady. "Wait, what?" asked Marge, looking shocked.

"And I said yes! Charlie wants me—oh, that kid wants me bad. Asked me to record a duet as soon as possible and wants me to feature in his next video. Laron said it'll probably be the biggest thing that hit the music business since sliced bread."

"I don't think sliced bread was ever part of the music industry," said Marge.

"Who cares? I'm going to be as big as Charlie, maybe even bigger! So how about them apples, huh?"

The others all exchanged worried glances, but Gran had already gotten up.

"You know what? I'm glad we had this little talk. I'm actually happy you finally came out and told me what you really think of me. You don't want me to be part of this family anymore? Good! I'm a disgrace to the Poole family name? Great! I've decided to change my name to Granny B, and I'm leaving this gang of rainers-on-parades for good. So consider this my resignation from this family. Goodbye and good riddance." And with these words, she stalked over to the door. Before she walked out, she turned and said, "And don't come crying to me when you're broke and miserable and I'm a multi-millionaire superstar with my own mansion in Calabasas, Cal. I won't pick up the phone!"

And then she was gone, slamming the door in the process.

*M*arge was staring out the kitchen window when Odelia walked up behind her. She put her hands on her mom's shoulders. "She'll be back," she said. "You know how she is. She gets these crazy ideas but before long she gets bored and then she'll come running."

"I don't know, Odelia," said Marge. "This time I have a feeling she might be gone for good. She's always had a thing for the glitz and glamour of celebrity life, and if this thing with Charlie Dieber works out she might move to the West Coast and never come back." She shook her head. "I was too hard on her. We were all too hard on her."

"But her performance was terrible. I thought a dose of reality would do her good."

Marge turned. "Your grandmother has never dealt with reality very well. And if this is her chance to escape reality once and for all, she'll grab it with both hands. Remember when she claimed to have been married to the most fascinating man in the world?"

"Yeah, but that fell through. And this will also fall through, and then she'll be back."

Marge returned to gazing out the window. "I've known your grandmother a lot longer than you have, and if there's one trait that's more dominant than all others, it's her stubbornness. That woman can be so mulish she'll drive you crazy."

"That means she'll drive Charlie Dieber crazy, and that Laron Weskit guy." Odelia gently massaged her mom's shoulders. "Besides, I'm sure she'll soon realize all the fame and glory in the world can never really replace a loving family. Plus, she'll miss her cats."

"Let's hope so. I'd hate to be the one to have driven your grandmother away."

Odelia returned to the living room, where her dad was watching *Jeopardy*. "Missing Gran already?" she asked as she took a seat beside him.

"Well, don't laugh but actually I do. That woman drives me nuts sometimes, but she also brings a lot of life into this household."

"She does, doesn't she?"

"I'm recording *Jeopardy*, by the way. And her favorite soaps. So when she comes back she can catch up. Otherwise I'll never hear the end of it."

"So you also think she'll be back soon?"

"Of course. This is her home, her family. I don't believe for a second she'd be willing to throw it all away to make a career as a pop star."

"Let's hope you're right," said Odelia, who was feeling a lot less sure already.

"So is it true the same goons that burgled your house tried to burgle the Hampton Cove Star?"

"Yeah, I'm starting to think Johnny and Jerry are not exactly the best burglars in the world. They keep getting caught, which is probably not how a good burglary should go."

"Well, as long as they're in jail, they won't be able to burgle anyone else."

"So how are you coping at the office? Don't you want to replace Gran? At least until she's back?" She knew how unreliable Gran could be when performing her duties as Dad's receptionist, and had often advised him to hire a regular receptionist. One he could count on. But Dad always said he liked Vesta sitting in that outer office, and scaring the hypochondriacs away. At least with her grumpy face there to greet them, only the patients who really needed a doctor managed to stick it out and stick around.

"Oh, don't you worry, honey, I'll manage," he said, affectionately patting his daughter's knee. "I tried to hire someone else, remember? That didn't work out too well, either."

"That's because you managed to hire the one person in Hampton Cove whom Gran hates even more than anyone else."

Dad had hired Scarlett Canyon for a while, Gran's mortal enemy, and that hadn't sat well with Gran at all. It also hadn't lasted. Before long, Gran had been back at the helm.

"Maybe I should call Vesta?" Tex suggested. "Ask her to reconsider?"

"I think it's best to leave her to stew in her own juices for a while. It's too soon to start begging her to come back. Besides, if you do that she'll be even more intolerable than usual. Best to wait a while, and let her realize she made a big mistake for herself."

"Maybe you're right," said her father. "You seem to know Vesta better than anyone."

Returning to her own home, she saw that her cats were all seated on the deck, holding some kind of meeting.

"Hey, you guys," she said, taking a seat next to them. "Everything all right?"

"I don't know, Odelia," said Max, usually the cats'

spokesperson. "We just feel we could have done so much more, if only those silly crooks hadn't interfered."

"Yeah, we're thinking about giving it another shot," said Harriet. "Return to the hotel and give those rooms another once-over."

"We never got the chance to search them properly," Brutus agreed.

"And maybe this time the rooms won't be burgled," said Dooley. "Unless that's a regular thing at the Hampton Cove Star."

Odelia laughed. "I don't think it's a regular thing, Dooley. But I also don't think it's a good idea to go back there now. The Weskits and Charlie will be in their rooms, and they'll notice the addition of four cats to their household. Besides, you had that chat with Cleo, didn't you? And she told you how she feels about Laron Weskit's involvement."

"Still, we've only scratched the surface," said Max.

"Yeah, we let you down, Odelia," said Harriet. "First with that silly show we gave, and then with that half-assed search. We haven't given you our best yet in this investigation, and we really want to make it up to you somehow."

She thought about that. "I'm not sure what else you can do. You've talked to Chickie's pets, you've talked to Laron Weskit's cat, I don't think there's a lot more you can do at this point." Nor, she felt, could she. She felt oddly stymied in this investigation. As if she was going around in circles and getting nowhere fast. And now this latest drama with Gran on top of everything else. She was losing her touch, and the fact that her cats had struck out only added to her general feeling of malaise.

"Let's not think about it anymore tonight," she said. "Let's all have a good night's sleep and I'm sure in the morning fresh ideas will come to us."

She got up, and headed into the house. Chase was cooking, which she found adorable. His specialty was spaghetti bolognese, though he was really outdoing himself now by going for a nice creamy lasagna. "Is it true that cats love lasagna?" he asked as he admired his own creation, then placed it in the oven.

"No, I think that's just a myth created by Jim Davis."

"Jim Davis?"

"The creator of Garfield."

"Okay. Well, I made extra, so if Max or the others fancy lasagna, there's plenty."

She took a seat on one of the high kitchen stools. "Do you think I'm losing my touch?"

"Losing your touch?" He walked around the kitchen counter and held out his hands. "Come here." They hugged and kissed, and she found him looking at her as if she were the dish of lasagna. "Um, no. In my expert opinion you haven't lost your touch, babe."

When she slapped him lightly on the chest, he laughed heartily.

"You know what I mean. I just feel I'm not getting anywhere with this investigation. As if I'm flailing around with no idea what the heck I'm doing."

"It's still early days. It could take weeks to figure out what exactly happened this morning. I'm going back there tomorrow first thing and have another chat with Tyson. I asked him to collect all the CCTV footage shot since last night, through the morning, and I'm going to watch it to see if there's any red flags. Maybe you can join me?"

"Watch security footage all day? No, thank you. I'd prefer to finally go and talk to Laron Weskit and the others."

"Oh, hasn't your uncle told you? The Mayor has extended his embargo. There will be no interviews of the Weskits or Dieber and Jamie for at least another day."

"What? But he can't do that!" She'd slipped off her stool

and threw up her hands in dismay. "They're important witnesses in a murder inquiry. Doesn't that take precedence over the Mayor's political games?"

"He argued they've been through enough, what with the burglary and all, and doesn't want them 'badgered' by the police—his words, not mine. He says that he talked to Laron about the whole Chickie thing and Laron assured him he's got nothing to do with that, and that he and his wife are as shocked and devastated as everyone else."

"Applesauce! They *have* to talk to the police."

"And sooner or later they will," Chase assured her. "They're not off the hook, Odelia."

"Yeah, but who knows what evidence they've been able to make disappear. Plus, they've had ample time to coordinate their stories, so whatever they'll tell you and Uncle Alec will just be the rehearsed story they want you to believe. The story they probably concocted with their legal team, to stay out of trouble as much as possible."

"Alec told me to back off. He doesn't want to go against the Mayor's wishes."

"God, this is making me sick."

"Listen," said Chase, placing plates and cutlery on place-mats. "Vesta is working with Laron and his team now, right? Can't you ask her to snoop around? Ask some questions?"

Odelia stared at her boyfriend. "That's brilliant!"

"Hey, I have my moments," said Chase with a grin.

But then Odelia's face fell. "I'll bet Gran won't talk to me, though. She's very upset."

"And I'll bet she will. You know what she's like. When it comes down to it, it's family first, always. And if she won't talk to you, for whatever silly reason, I'll have a crack at her. She's always liked me."

Odelia smiled. "I dare you to call Gran and to recruit her as a police spy inside Laron Weskit's operation."

"You're on," said Chase, and took out his phone. Moments later Gran picked up.

"Oh, hey, Vesta," said Chase, giving Odelia a wink. "I wanna ask you a big favor."

26

We still strongly felt as if we'd let Odelia down. So the four of us agreed to return to the hotel as soon as the house was quiet, and see if we couldn't have another look at those hotel rooms.

"Odelia is counting on us," said Dooley.

"Yes, she is," Brutus agreed. "But she's simply too nice to tell us how she really feels. How we all let her down terribly."

"I think we owe it to her to give it another shot," said Harriet.

We were all in agreement. And so it was decided. The moment Odelia and Chase were sound asleep we all snuck out of the house and set paw for downtown Hampton Cove, where the Hampton Cove Star awaited. Unfortunately Odelia had retrieved the keycards she'd given us, so we wouldn't be able to use them to get in. But we're cats. Somehow or other we always manage to get where we need to be.

So we trudged along the sidewalk, the hour long past midnight, and soon found ourselves in the heart of town. Across the street from the Star is Kingman's General Store,

146

though I should probably say Kingman's human's General Store. Of course at this time of night the store was closed, and of Kingman there was no sign.

"Probably in the park for cat choir," said Dooley, following my gaze.

"They'll all be in the park for cat choir," said Harriet. "Except for me, and to be absolutely honest, I'll probably never go to cat choir again."

"But why, sugar biscuit?" asked Brutus. "I thought you did pretty well tonight."

"Didn't you see the horrified looks on people's faces? And didn't you hear the laughter when my performance was over? They hated me—probably thought it was the most ridiculous thing they'd ever seen or heard."

"I don't think so, snow bunny. I think they were surprised, that's all. They've never seen that kind of performance before. And you know what people are like. They hate whatever's new—at least at first. But give them some time and they'll appreciate your performance for what it was: refreshing and adorable."

"Oh, Brutus, my snickerdoodle, you always know exactly what to say to cheer me up." Then her shoulders sagged. "But I still think it was terrible, and by now word will have spread through Hampton Cove's cat community and soon they'll all be laughing like hyenas. No, I'm never going to cat choir again and that's my final word."

We'd been staring up at the hotel while Harriet shared her self-critique with us, and suddenly I was struck by an idea. "Why don't we try the fire escape?" Once, not all that long ago, Dooley and I had managed to get into the hotel that way.

And so we quickly crossed the road, ducked into a side alley and arrived at the back of the hotel. And there, gleaming and majestic, was a metal fire escape. We scaled the wire mesh staircase and soon arrived on the fourth-floor platform. Unfortunately it was one of those doors that only open from the inside, with a push bar. And since there was no one to push on this particular bar, we were stuck. But then Harriet decided to use her secret weapon: a repeat performance of tonight's song, and this time we were four, not two, with Dooley, myself and Brutus provided backing vocals.

It must have made quite an impression, for very quickly a window to one of the rooms opened and a shoe whizzed through the night and hit me smack in the head.

"Ouch!" I said.

But seeing as this appeared to be the price to pay for achieving greatness, I didn't let up and kept on howling away. More windows opened, and more shoes zoomed through the air. Few of them hit their targets, except a big boot that hit Brutus in the back.

"Hey, watch it, you brute!" he yelled.

And then, finally, the moment we'd all been waiting for arrived: a sleepy-looking little girl opened the door. Rubbing her eyes, she said, "Mommy? It's the cat from the show."

"Come back to bed, honey," a woman's voice sounded from halfway down the hallway.

"But it's the pretty white cat from the show, mommy. And she's singing again." She bent over and petted Harriet, who purred up a storm in response.

"Annabella! Back to bed!" the same voice came back, and Annabella, after a moment's hesitation—the sight of Harriet, a star performer, was clearly very enticing—she ran along to her mother. Soon all was quiet once more. Except this time the door was open, and so we quickly entered.

"Great work, angel bunny," said Brutus. "You nailed it."

"I think I'm improving, though, don't you think?" said Harriet.

"With leaps and bounds," said her ever-loyal boyfriend.

"I think our backing vocals made a big impression, too," said Dooley.

"For which I thank you guys," said Harriet.

We'd arrived at the Weskits' room and I had a flash of déjà-vu. Once again we needed to get inside.

"Room service!" said Brutus suddenly.

We all looked up at this.

"Come again?" I said.

He pointed to the same cart Dooley and I had employed before, and repeated, "Room service. These rich and famous people never sleep. Instead they spend half the night ordering room service. So if we can sneak onto one of these room service carts while they're being ridden into the room, we're golden."

"Are you quite sure about this?" asked Harriet after we'd been waiting in that hallway for fifteen minutes with not a room service person in sight.

I felt she was right to be impatient. The hotel seemed pretty quiet. The only person we'd seen was a man staggering down the corridor, giving us curious looks. He'd muttered, "Eight cats—what do you know?" but had still managed to enter his room.

"Sure I'm sure," said Brutus, though he sounded a lot less sure than when he'd first made the suggestion. Problem was, neither of us had a better idea.

Another ten minutes later, though, the elevator dinged, and much to our elation a room service cart, pushed by a room service person, came squeaking down the corridor.

"Now!" cried Brutus. "Go, go, go!"

And so we all hopped onto the lower platform of the cart, nicely obscured by a sheet, and hoped we'd caught the right bus. Otherwise we'd be locked up in the wrong room.

The squeak-squeak-squeak of the wheels suddenly halted, a deferential knock sounded, followed by an equally deferential cough, and the door opened. Slippered feet appeared in our field of vision. They were pale and bony, and unfortunately—my knowledge of human legs is extensive but still limited to the few humans whose sticks for legs I've made an acquaintance with over the years—I had no way of knowing whether they were Laron Weskit's or his wife's, or indeed The Dieber's or Jamie's.

"Are those the right legs?" asked Harriet, wrestling with the same vexing question.

"I don't know!" said Brutus, sounding panicky.

"We need to be sure!" she hissed.

"It's all right," said Dooley, and we all turned to stare at him, inasmuch as we were able to, considering we didn't have a lot of space on that cart's lower level.

"Is it Laron Weskit?" I asked.

"Trust me, we're fine," was the only thing he allowed himself to divulge.

The cart was wheeled in, and the door closed behind us. We were in the lion's den.

I was too nervous to jump out from our hiding place, but not Dooley. The moment the door fell into its lock he slipped down from the cart.

"Dooley!" I said. "Wait!"

But I could hear Dooley's voice clearly say, "It's so great to see you again!"

Suddenly the veil was lifted and we found ourselves staring into the familiar face of... Grandma Muffin!

*G*ran carefully listened to our story. We'd all taken a seat in the salon, while Dooley had jumped up on her lap and was purring contentedly while she caressed him. Dooley is, after all, Gran's, and had probably missed her.

"I'm sorry for walking out on you like that," said Gran. "But these people really drive me crazy sometimes. I know my show wasn't the best it could be and all that, but it was something, and several people came up to me and told me how fresh and exciting they found it. Revolutionary, one man said. Just what we need in a world obsessed with youth and beauty—though I'm not sure if I should take that as a compliment or an insult. But Marge and Alec dismissed everything I said out of hand. And I don't think that's fair, so I wanted to teach them a lesson, and now here I am."

"And here we are, too," said Dooley happily.

"Do you have to pay for this room yourself, Gran?" I asked.

"No, as a matter of fact I don't. Laron Weskit is paying for it out of his own pocket, and tomorrow morning we're going to discuss the terms of my contract. And Charlie wants to discuss our duet. So you see? I'm not delusional. I have a talent, and at least these professional people appreciate it."

"But you are coming back to us at some point, aren't you, Gran?" asked Harriet.

"Yeah, we miss you," said Brutus.

"Of course I'm coming back, but first I want to show the family what I can do. That dear old Gran has a lot more going for her than just good looks and devastating charm."

"So can you do it?" I asked. "Can you smuggle us into the Weskits' room?"

"Sure. But maybe not tonight. Let's give it a shot first thing tomorrow morning. When they're all downstairs for breakfast you can search those rooms to your heart's content."

"Thanks, Gran," I said.

"Though I don't know what you're hoping to accomplish, to be honest," she said. "Laron doesn't strike me as a murderer, and neither does his wife. And as far as Charlie and Jamie are concerned, they're the sweetest couple you could ever hope to meet."

"So they're not killers, either," I said, nodding.

"Nope. You never know, of course. Looks can be deceiving, and even though I'm probably the world's best judge of character, even I can be deceived, though I doubt it."

"Tex says he misses you," I said. "And so do Marge and Odelia."

"And Chase," said Brutus.

"Talking about Chase, he recruited me," said Gran with a smile. "Asked me to snoop around and find out what's cooking in the Weskits' kitchen."

"They have their own kitchen?" asked Dooley, wide-eyed.

"Chase wants me to ask them a couple of questions," Gran

said, petting Dooley on the head. "Act as his eyes and ears because the Mayor has told the police to stand down."

"Do you miss your family, too, Gran?" asked Harriet now.

"Of course! I miss all of you. And I'm really glad you decided to pay me a visit."

"So are you going to do what Chase asked you to do?" I asked.

"Sure, why not? But I told him the same thing I just told you: I don't think Laron is the guy. But of course I can't prove that until I get to know him a little better. And now that you're all here, we can work together to prove that my new friends had nothing to do with Chickie Hay's murder. Can you do that for me?"

"Yes, Gran!" we all spoke in chorus. Though I had no idea what she'd actually asked us to do. Regardless, if there was anything to be found, we'd find it. I was sure of it. Or at least as sure as Gran seemed to be of her boundless talent to entertain Spotify listeners.

We spent the night in Gran's room, which was spacious and pleasant and warm, and she even ordered room service for us: extra-delicious kibble and extra-yummy soft food.

"You know, Max?" said Dooley as we tucked in, "I think I could get used to this life."

"What life, Dooley?" I asked as I gobbled up a kernel of kibble.

"The life of the rich and famous," he said. "Room service at all hours of the day and night, a nice suite to lounge around in, a flock of adoring fans…"

We all pricked up our ears when loud singing came from outside. When Gran opened her window something was thrown in her face. A pair of panties. She stared at it for a moment, then threw them back. "Wrong room!" she yelled, and slammed the window.

"I think those were meant for Charlie," said Brutus with a laugh.

"Damn cheek," Grandma grumbled, and decided to call it a night. We all curled up on the huge and comfy bed, and moments later only the sounds of one old lady and four cats snoring softly could be heard.

The next morning, we discovered the pleasures of room service all over again, and once more were pleased with the selection of tasty chicken nuggets at our disposal.

"I'm going downstairs to have breakfast with the others," said Gran after taking a shower. She was dressed in a nice new dress I'd never seen before. It was short and sexy.

When she caught us all staring at her, she twirled around, and said, "Laron got these for me last night, from the hotel shop. Nice, huh? And Shannon Weskit is taking me shopping later. They want me decked out in a completely fresh set of threads." She sighed, her eyes shining with delight. "A girl could get used to this life, that's for sure," she said, echoing Dooley's words from the night before.

Before she went down for breakfast, she instructed us to follow her out into the hallway, and stay close to the wall. She then knocked on Laron Weskit's door, and when he opened we all quickly scooted between his legs and into his room.

"Ready for breakfast, Laron?" we could hear Gran ask, and Laron grumbled something in response. Clearly he was not a morning person.

"Gran is in better shape than this Laron guy!" said Dooley, and we all giggled at that.

We'd immediately streaked underneath the bed, where we now remained hidden until the coast was clear. Finally Laron and Shannon left, and the room was finally ours.

"Hey, intruders," said suddenly a familiar voice.

When we turned, we found ourselves being addressed by the hairless cat Cleo.

"Cleo!" cried Dooley. "So nice to see you again!"

"Likewise, furball," said Cleo, obviously in a great mood. "And who are these guys? I briefly saw you last night but we weren't properly introduced."

"This is Harriet, and this is Brutus. Harriet and Brutus, meet Cleo, Laron's cat."

"Nice to meet you," said Brutus politely.

"Aren't you the singer from last night?" Cleo asked Harriet.

Harriet perked up at this. "Did you see my show?"

"I wasn't lucky enough to catch it live, but Laron and Shannon watched the footage on the big screen after you guys had all left."

"And? What did you think?" asked Harriet, sounding a little nervous.

"Loved it, sister! And so did Laron and Shannon. They thought you were fantastic!"

"Oh, my," said Harriet, visibly touched. "Oh, my, oh, my."

"You're the real thing, girl," said Cleo. "And those are not my words but Laron's. You know he's a record executive, right? If he says you'll hit it big, you better pay attention."

"Did you hear that, Brutus? They loved us! Loved us!"

"That's wonderful news, chocolate drop," said Brutus, though he didn't look as happy as I would have expected. And as Harriet chatted some more with Cleo, who turned out to be a big fan, I took Brutus aside.

"Everything all right, buddy? You don't look so happy."

"Can't you see what's happening, Max?" he asked with a pained look on his face.

"Um… Harriet is being showered with compliments and you're jealous? Is that it?"

"No! She's getting showered with compliments and soon

155

she'll start a big career and where does that leave me? Nowhere!"

"But you'll still be her backing vocalist, right?"

"No! Well, maybe at first, but everybody knows backing vocalists are replaceable. Here today, gone tomorrow. Soon she'll have admirers all over the world, and she'll fall for one of them, and then she'll forget all about me. Just you wait and see. It'll happen."

"I don't think so," I said. "Even if Harriet makes it big— and that's still a very big if—she'll take you with her, all the way to the top. I'm absolutely sure of it."

"Didn't you ever see the *Hunger Games?*" he asked sadly.

"Um… yeah, I seem to remember I did. But what's that got to do with anything?"

"You know how that ended, right?"

"Um…" I didn't really see the connection, and I told him.

"She dumps the boy she knew from back home! One of the Hemsworth brothers. She dumps the Hemsworth when she gets the hots for the new kid she meets on the road. And that's exactly what's going to happen with me and Harriet." His shoulders slumped, and no matter how much I tried to cheer him up, he wouldn't hear of it. He said he was a Hemsworth now, and soon Harriet would meet her Peeta and that would be the end of it.

Still, we had a job to do, so while Brutus pined, and Harriet giggled at Cleo's compliments, Dooley and I started a thorough search of the Weskits' hotel room.

"What are we looking for, exactly, Max?" asked Dooley, and not unreasonably so.

"Um…" I would have said the murder weapon, but with strangulation the murder weapon is actually a pair of hands, and it wasn't likely we would find those lying around.

"You'll know it when you find it," I told him, remembering Odelia's words.

He repeated these words to himself like a mantra, and then we started snooping around in earnest. I checked every possible square inch of that room, and when we were done I had to admit there wasn't a thing that really jumped out at me. I knew that Mrs. Weskit loved shopping, as I'd found a massive amount of shopping bags, most of them still unpacked and all with names of boutiques and shoe shops printed on them. I also knew Mr. Weskit loved cufflinks. He had an entire collection and appeared to take them with him on the road. There was also a dressing room stashed with shirts, pants, socks, ties for him and blouses, skirts, dresses and shoes, shoes, shoes for her. But nothing that told me that either of these people was the cold-blooded killer of Miss Chickie Hay.

When Dooley and I met up again in the living room, he shook his head. "I found a book about having babies. It was next to the toilet. Does that tell you anything, Max?"

"It tells me the Weskits may be thinking about family expansion," I said, "but apart from that not much more."

"I also found a greeting card sent by Chickie Hay to Laron. It said something about eternal friendship and loving affection. Dated three years ago."

"So three years ago they were still friends. I wonder what happened to make them fall out like this."

"We'd have to ask Laron."

"Gran will have to ask Laron, and I'm sure she will."

"Over breakfast? Do you think that'll work?"

"Humans love breakfast, Dooley. Especially the breakfast buffet at a five-star hotel. If there are any secrets the Weskits are liable to spill, they'll spill them over breakfast."

Harriet was still talking about herself, and how great she was, and the more she talked the more Brutus gnawed his claws, looking terrified at the prospect of being Hemsworthed. There wasn't a lot I could do for him, to be honest. If Harriet was going to Hemsworth him, she would. But she wasn't there yet, and frankly I didn't think she'd ever be there. These celebrity types talk a good game, but often fail at follow-through.

"Let's start on the next room," I told Dooley. We both looked a little wearily at the door to Charlie and Jamie's room, which was open. Searching a room is a lot of work, especially if you're a cat and you're hampered by the lack of opposable thumbs to open cabinets and drawers and such. Still, we managed, and over the course of the next half hour we took a deep dive into the private life of The Dieber. Finally I admitted defeat.

"Nothing," I said when I met Dooley again.

"I think I may have found something, Max," he said, and led me deeper into the bedroom the couple shared. There, hidden underneath the bed, was a letter. I plunked down to read it, and soon was smiling from ear to ear.

"You did it, Dooley," I said.

"I did?" he asked, a smile spreading across his features.

"You solved the murder!"

Now all we had to do was get this letter out of that room and into Gran's hands.

2 8

When Vesta saw the breakfast buffet she nearly swooned. She'd always been a big fan of breakfast buffets, and one of the things she liked most about going on holiday was staying in hotels with a big breakfast spread. The dining room was bright and airy, and smelled of freshly brewed coffee, freshly baked pastry and freshly squeezed orange juice. She hurried over to the buffet, picked up a tray, and soon was loading up on croissants, muffins, toast, scrambled eggs, those delicious little sausages and yummy spring rolls.

By the time she returned to her table, the eyes of the others were on her tray and Laron had to laugh. In spite of what his semi-permanent frown indicated, the man had a pleasant laugh. "Vesta! You can't possibly eat all of that!"

"Watch me," she growled, and plunked down her tray.

Across from her sat Charlie and Jamie, the lovey-dovey couple, although from the looks of things Jamie wasn't as lovey-dovey this morning as usual.

"That tribute song for Chickie you sang last night was

beautiful," Vesta told the young woman, deciding to get the ball rolling and see what the outcome was.

Jamie gave her a sweet smile and swept her long auburn tresses over her shoulder. "Thanks, Mrs. Muffin. I thought it was only fitting, us being best friends and all."

"Terrible loss," said Laron, shaking his head. "Absolutely terrible."

"Do they know who did it yet?" asked Charlie, removing an arm that seemed to be permanently glued in place on his girlfriend's back to pick up a bread roll and start picking at it without much excitement.

"No, not a clue," said Vesta.

"Oh, that's right," said Shannon. "You're familiar with the way the police work in this town, aren't you?"

"Yeah, my son is chief of police," she said. "And so far he's got nothing. Zip."

"Too bad."

"Yeah, if he doesn't get results soon they're calling in the state police," said Vesta, watching carefully how the others responded. Apart from a raised eyebrow from Shannon, there was no response. Either these were some very cool cucumbers or they had no clue about what had happened.

"I think it was probably a prowler," said Laron. "Has to be. They're always attracted to people with money. He came in, bumped into Chickie, and that was her fate sealed."

"You mean like the men who broke into your room last night?" asked Charlie.

"Sure. Wouldn't surprise me if it was the same ones. Only time will tell, though."

"They do have one man in custody," said Shannon as she took a sip from her herbal tea. "A superfan. In other words, a stalker."

"Yeah, I think I heard something about that."

"He's not a serious suspect, though," said Vesta. "No

motive, for one thing. I mean, he's her self-declared number-one fan. Why would he go and choke her to death?"

"Mental health issues?" said Shannon. "Happens more than you know. Most of these stalkers are sick in the head, Vesta."

"Did Chickie ever mention anyone threatening her?" asked Gran.

Shannon shook her head. "Last time I talked to her she was the one threatening me."

"She was a tough cookie," her husband agreed.

"What did she threaten you about?" asked Gran.

"Oh, this and that," said Shannon vaguely.

"She was upset that I refused to sell her back the rights to her music," said Laron. "But why should I? She was the one leaving me, and signing with another company. So why should I hand her back her music with a nice bow on top? That's not how it works."

"You were going to hand the rights back to her, though, isn't that right, Laron?" asked Charlie.

"Yeah, for the right price. Not the peanuts she was prepared to pay for it."

"We were in the middle of negotiations, and at this point the lawyers had taken over," said Shannon.

"Too bad," said Charlie. "She was one talented lady."

Jamie had been conspicuously silent, but now burst out, "She wasn't that talented, Charlie. All of her greatest hits were written by other people, and the few songs she wrote herself didn't do well."

"Yeah, but at least she wrote some of her own stuff," said Charlie, clearly taken aback by this sudden outburst. "Most singers don't write anything. They all buy songs from professional songwriters."

"Oh, so now you're having a go at me, are you?"

"No, I didn't mean—"

"Okay, so I don't write my own music. That doesn't make me a lesser singer, does it?"

"No, of course not. I just wanted to—"

"Oh, forget about it," said Jamie, and promptly got up and stormed off, her face a thundercloud.

Uh-oh, thought Vesta. The cats were probably still upstairs, snooping around.

"Excuse me," she said. "Have to powder my nose." And she quickly got up and went in pursuit of Charlie's girlfriend.

She saw her entering the elevator and cursed under her breath. Then her eye fell on the staircase. Taking a deep breath, she waltzed into the stairwell, and started mounting the stairs as quickly as she could. In spite of her age she was in excellent fettle, the advantage of working as a doctor's receptionist—and when she exited the stairwell on the fourth floor saw Jamie as she placed her keycard against the door and opened it.

"Jamie, hold up!" Vesta yelled, and hurried over.

"What is it?" asked Jamie, none too friendly.

"I'm sorry. You'll probably think me some gossipy old lady, but it pains me to see a beautiful young couple like you and Charlie going through a bad patch. I can tell how much Charlie loves you, and you're clearly very fond of him, so…"

Jamie's pout intensified. "He had no business telling me singers who write their own material are superior to singers that don't. Lots of artists buy their songs, and does anyone call them out for it? No, they don't. Charlie himself doesn't write his own stuff."

"I'm sure he didn't mean it like that," said Vesta, raising her voice so her cats, if they were still inside, could get the hell out of there.

"No need to shout," said Jamie, still pouting.

"Oh, I'm sorry. I'm a little hard of hearing, and you know how it is, you start to talk louder because you think everybody is hard of hearing. Look, if you want my advice, I don't think Charlie meant anything by what he said. He's obviously crazy about you."

"I guess so," said the girl, who was, Vesta now realized, very young indeed. Maybe not even twenty yet.

"Lighten up a little, honey," said Vesta, adopting a motherly tone. "Life is too short to make a mountain out of every molehill, and your relationship will only suffer."

"I know. It's just that… he drives me crazy sometimes. He's so annoying, you know?"

"That's because you've been cooped up together in here for too long. Maybe you should go for a walk. Get some fresh air."

She nodded. "Maybe I will. It's true that Charlie and I have spent an awful lot of time together. And maybe I need to clear my head. Thank you, Mrs. Muffin. You're very kind."

"You're welcome, Jamie. And it's Vesta."

And as Jamie passed into her room, Vesta glanced beyond her, and could just see Dooley's tail as it disappeared into the next room.

Phew. Saved by the bell.

Vesta made her way down again—this time taking the elevator—and hoped her cats had found something useful. When she joined the others she was gratified to see that her tray hadn't been cleaned away. So she sat down, and dedicated herself to the consumption of the best breakfast she'd had in a long time, from time to time directing a question at her messmates, and Laron in particular, who she felt had the most to gain from Chickie's death. But no matter what question she lobbed at the guy, he always had his answer ready.

But if he hadn't killed Chickie Hay, then who had?

29

*J*amie closed the door and immediately walked over to the bedroom. How could she have been so stupid to leave that letter lying around? With the police searching high and low. Laron had told them the police wouldn't touch them—that he'd used his influence with the Mayor to call off the dogs—but she knew that was only a momentary reprieve. Sooner or later they would be interrogated, and if they found that letter in her room...

She dove under the bed and her heart stopped when she discovered the letter gone.

Oh, no!

Had Charlie found it? But if he had, he would have told her about it. He'd found religion, and honesty was part of his new deal. At first his religious fervor had been fun and refreshing. Now it irked her that every time something was on his mind he'd start yapping about it. A good relationship could only survive if you kept a couple of secrets from your partner, but that wasn't how Charlie thought about it at all. Or his pastor.

She searched her memory. Where could that letter be?

She'd been reading it last night, but then Charlie had suddenly come into the room and she'd had to drop it to the floor, where it had remained. She'd intended to pick it up and hide it but hadn't had the chance. And now with that nosy old lady going on and on about the investigation, clearly a spy for her chief of police son, she'd felt the sudden urge to go back for that letter and destroy it. No good could ever come of anyone reading its content. No good at all.

She looked around, then pensively walked into the living area of their suite. And then she saw that the connecting door was ajar. Could it be… She quickly opened it and glanced around Laron and Shannon's room. And that's when she saw it: a cat's tail, disappearing into the bedroom. Could Cleo have stolen her letter? Were cats that smart?

She stepped into the bedroom and found five pairs of eyes staring back at her. She recognized that horrible hairless cat of Shannon's… and the four cats from last night. Vesta's cats. And one of those cats had her letter clasped between its teeth.

"Give me that, you stupid beast," she said, and lunged for the dumb animal.

The cat was quicker, of course, and leaped out of the way.

And thus began a chase around the suite: Jamie bigger and more determined, but the cat more agile and a lot faster. Sooner or later she'd corner the stupid mongrel though.

"Give me my letter!" she screamed when she had the animal cornered under the bed. But the moment she reached out a hand to grab it, it scooted out the other side.

She practically howled with frustration. "Get back here, you horrible beast!"

And then she had it: the mongrel had run into the bathroom. "Ha!" she yelled. "Not very smart, cat!"

She grabbed a bathrobe from a hook and proceeded slowly into the bathroom.

The animal sat behind the toilet, eyeing her with fear in its eyes. "Good. You should be afraid!" she shouted. "Cause when I get you, I'm going to skin you alive!"

But just then, something jumped onto her back, and moments later she howled in pain as she felt claws digging in!

She reached back to get the thing off her but it hissed and dug its claws in deeper!

"Get off me!" she screeched. "Get off, get off, get off!"

She swung around and the cat went flying and hit the wall, then dropped into the bathtub with a clunking sound. It was big and fat and red—a monstrous beast.

The gray cat, meanwhile, had escaped from behind the toilet and now raced back into the other room. Jamie descended upon the cat that had clawed her, and picked it up by the scruff of the neck. God, it was heavy. It was also hissing and twisting, to no avail.

Oh, how she hated cats—and after today she'd hate the foul breed even more.

"I'll teach you a lesson you won't forget," she said, and grabbed one of Shannon's hairbrushes from the sink. "I'll teach you to mutilate my back with those filthy claws."

She'd moved back into the living space and raised the brush to give the cat a good thrashing. Just then, the door to the room burst open and Laron and Shannon stood before her, Vesta and Charlie right behind them.

"What the hell are you doing with that cat?!" Shannon cried, outrage written all over her features.

"Nothing, I swear!" she said as she dropped both cat and hairbrush. "That cat over there stole... stole something from me!"

To her horror she saw that the small gray cat had jumped into Vesta's arms and that the old lady was carefully taking the letter from between the cat's teeth and started reading it.

"That's mine!" she yelled. "Give it back! It's mine!"

But Vesta looked up at her, a hint of steel in her eyes. "I think it's time I called my son," she said. "Laron, Shannon, grab her and make sure she doesn't escape. I think we just caught Chickie's killer."

30

*O*delia, who was at the office, was surprised to get the call. When she arrived at the hotel she was even more surprised to find her four cats, all looking fairly triumphant.

"How did you guys get here?" she asked, crouching down.

"We felt we hadn't done enough," said Max.

"Yeah, we let you down, Odelia," Harriet added. "So we decided to search those rooms again."

"And Dooley found something. Gran says it proves that Jamie is the killer."

She straightened and watched as Jamie Borowiak was led out of the hotel by two of her uncle's officers, cuffed and looking distinctly distraught.

"I didn't do it," the young woman said tearfully. "I had nothing to do with this."

"Tell that to the judge," one of the officers snapped.

Behind Jamie, Chase now also walked out, followed by Uncle Alec and Gran.

"What's going on?" asked Odelia. "Why did you arrest Jamie?"

"Look at this," said her uncle, and produced a letter wrapped in a plastic cover.

She quickly read through its contents. It was a letter written by Chickie Hay, only a week ago, addressed to Jamie. It basically accused Jamie of stealing her boyfriend Charlie Dieber away from her, and warned her that she would take sweet, sweet revenge.

"There's nothing new in this letter," she said. "We already knew they had a fight."

But Gran tapped the document. "Jamie tried very hard to hide this letter. She chased Dooley all around the room and practically murdered Max when he tried to protect his friend. Why would she go to all that trouble if she wasn't the killer?"

"Because she didn't want people to know about the rift between her and Chickie?"

"Chickie was threatening Jamie with 'sweet, sweet revenge,'" Gran said stubbornly. "So Jamie decided to shut her up once and for all. It's all in the letter, Odelia."

"But it's not, is it?"

Gran brought her face close to Odelia's, noses touching. "Read. Between. The. Lines."

"I think it's pretty conclusive," said Uncle Alec. "And I'm sure we'll get a confession."

"Dooley found this letter?" asked Odelia, glancing down at Dooley, who looked proud as a peacock.

"Yeah," said Gran. "I managed to smuggle the cats into Laron and Shannon's room, and Dooley found the letter lying under Jamie's bed. She must have realized she dropped the letter cause she came back to look for it, but by that time Dooley had already snatched it between his teeth. She then chased poor Dooley all across the room, until we happened to arrive and saved him and the incriminating letter in the nick of time."

"Good job, Ma," said Uncle Alec in a rare compliment, and gave his mother a peck on the cheek.

The old lady looked pleased as punch. "I think this might hamper my chances for that duet with Charlie, though," she said. "I doubt he'll want to work with the woman who put his girlfriend in jail."

"Yeah, Laron already told me in no uncertain terms what he felt about your latest stunt," said Uncle Alec.

"He did, did he? Well, did you tell him his protégée is a killer?"

"I told him we arrested Jamie and he said he'd get the best damn lawyer in the country and I'd be sorry and you would be, too."

"Yikes. I'm quaking in my boots," said Gran with a grin.

"Do you guys want a lift home?" Odelia asked her cats.

"No, I think we'll stick around for a bit," said Max.

"You did great," she said, and squeezed Dooley's cheeks. He giggled.

"I think my career will be over, too," said Harriet a little ruefully. "Laron will never engage one of the cats that got Jamie sent to prison."

"Oh, well, you had a good run," said Brutus, looking very pleased all of a sudden.

A crowd of onlookers had gathered, and watched as Jamie was placed in the back of a squad car and driven off. Several people stood pointing up at the hotel, holding their smartphones to take pictures. And when Odelia looked up she saw Laron Weskit standing in front of his hotel room window, accompanied by Shannon and Charlie. They didn't look happy, and moved away from the window, not wanting to be filmed.

"Dark days," said Odelia as Chase joined her. "At least for the Weskits."

"And Charlie," said Chase. "He just watched his girlfriend being arrested for murder."

"Do you think she did it?"

"Don't you?" he deflected.

"I don't know. That letter doesn't prove anything, does it? I mean, so Chickie wrote a letter, promising revenge for stealing her boyfriend. I'm sure that's just the language of a woman scorned. And I doubt Jamie would kill Chickie just because of that threat."

"Yes, but why did she try so hard to make that letter disappear?"

"But she didn't, did she? According to Dooley the letter was just lying there, under the bed. It's only when Gran started asking questions that she decided the letter wasn't fit for public consumption and should stay private."

"Let's see what she says. I'm sure your uncle will be able to get the truth out of her."

"I guess."

"And at the very least she deserves to be punished for treating your cats the way she did. She was just about to give Max a beating with a hairbrush."

Odelia raised an eyebrow. "She was?"

"Yeah, that's what your grandmother says, and Jamie is not denying it."

"Maybe you're right. Maybe she does deserve to be punished."

If there was one thing Odelia hated above all else, it was people who tormented animals. As far as she was concerned, the punishment couldn't be big enough.

"**W**hat's going on?" asked Kingman when we joined him.

"Oh, just that Dooley managed to catch a killer," I said.

Kingman stared from me to Dooley. "Dooley caught a killer? How did that happen?"

"I found an inseminating piece of evidence," said Dooley happily.

"Not inseminating, incriminating," Harriet corrected him.

"Very incriminating," I said. "A letter Chickie Hay wrote Jamie Borowiak, threatening revenge for stealing her boyfriend Charlie Dieber."

"And that letter proves that she killed her?" asked Kingman.

"It does. Convulsively," said Dooley, still beaming.

"Conclusively," I said.

"Well, congratulations, Dooley," said Kingman. "You must feel like a real star now."

"A star detective," said Dooley with a smile.

"I'm just glad this investigation is over," said Brutus. "I feel very tired all of a sudden."

"It's these celebrities," said Harriet. "They're very tiring."

She seemed a little downcast now that her big career was over even before it began.

"So what's going to happen now?" asked Kingman.

"Now Uncle Alec is going to interrogate Jamie and then once she confesses she's going to appear before the judge and then she'll go to prison," said Dooley, the expert.

"No, I mean what's going to happen with you? Are you going to have to testify in court? Usually the people who find important evidence, especially of the incriminating kind, have to testify in court, in front of a judge and a jury of their peers."

"A jury of our peers would be a jury of cats," Harriet pointed out. "I don't think that's ever going to happen."

"No, I don't think Dooley will have to testify in court," I agreed. "Cats rarely testify in court."

"Rarely? You mean never," said Harriet. "It's not fair but there you are. We never get to testify in court, and we never get to go to court against anyone, either."

"Who would you like to take to court, Harriet?" asked Kingman, an amused expression on his face.

"Where do I start? I wouldn't mind taking Shanille to court, for instance. She told me last week that I can't sing solos anymore. Which I thought was extremely unfair."

"Why can't you sing solos anymore?" asked Dooley, interested in Harriet's latest drama.

"She feels that the whole idea of singing solos is anti-democratic. It breeds jealousy and discord in cat choir and she can't have that. So from now on no more solos."

Which was probably the reason Harriet was so keen on starting her career as a singer on stage. To get back at Shanille. Show her once and for all what a terrific soloist she really was.

"I doubt whether a jury would convict Shanille for that,"

said Kingman. "Denying a choir singer their solo is not a punishable offense, as far as I know."

"Well, it should be," Harriet insisted. "It's caused me great emotional distress and I'm entitled compensation. Not to mention she's reduced my earning capacity. A talent scout who just happened to be watching our rehearsals would have signed me up in a heartbeat. But if no one is allowed to sing a solo, no scouts will come to our rehearsals."

"Do you really think talent scouts come to our rehearsals?" I asked.

"Of course! How else are they going to scout fresh new talent like me?"

Kingman, who'd been smiling at this quaint conceit, wiped the smile from his face when he caught Harriet's icy glare. It never ends well when you laugh at something she says. Harriet hates to be made a fool of, a chink in her armor we're all well aware of.

"So are you going to do any more performing?" asked Kingman now.

"I doubt it," said Harriet sadly. "Laron fired Gran, and I guess that means the end of my career, too."

"Too bad," muttered Brutus, though he looked like the cat that got the cream.

"Maybe I'll have a word with Shanille," said Kingman. "Ask her to reconsider this whole solo policy. I'll tell her that every great choir embraces the solo as part of its repertoire, and if she simply promises every member of cat choir that they are entitled to perform their own solo at some point, it shouldn't breed any jealousy or envy."

"That's a great idea, Kingman," I said. "If everyone is a soloist, there's no need for jealousy."

Harriet didn't look convinced. "It will devalue the solo, though," she said. "If everyone is a soloist, what's the point? Besides, cat choir has dozens of members. If they all get to do a solo, it will take months before it's my turn. I think this is a lousy idea, Kingman."

And on this note of constructive criticism, she stalked off, then turned. "Let's go, Brutus." And Brutus, after waggling his eyebrows at us, quickly traipsed off after her.

"Tough baby," said Kingman.

"Harriet wants to shine," I explained. "And it's hard to shine when everyone shines."

"I would like to do a solo once," said Dooley.

Kingman and I both smiled. Now that Dooley had tasted stardom, he wanted more.

"I'll talk to Shanille," said Kingman. "Tonight you'll get your solo, Dooley."

And Dooley shone, which warmed my heart. The thing is, some cats are pleased when other cats shine. Dooley being a star made me feel happy for him, not jealous. Then again, Dooley was my friend, of course. I doubted whether I'd feel happy if, for instance, Milo ended up being the star of the piece, as I don't like Milo all that much.

"So are you guys going to the wake?" asked Kingman.

We both stared at him. "Wake? What wake?" I asked.

"Chickie Hay's wake, of course. Who else? Wilbur is going, and so is half the town. Wilbur said it'll be the social event of the season."

Wilbur Vickery, Kingman's human, is as much a gossip as his four-legged sidekick.

"What's a wake, Max?" asked Dooley.

"It's when people get to greet the body of a dearly departed," I said. "They can sit with the body and remember their loved one, or even share stories about the deceased."

"Why is it called a wake, though?"

"Because you have to stay awake throughout the thing," said Kingman. "If you fall asleep it's a sign of disrespect."

I doubted whether this was the case, but Dooley seemed

satisfied. "I hope I can stay awake," he said. "I wouldn't want to be disrespectful to Miss Hay."

"I'm sure we're not invited," I said, "so that won't be an issue."

"And I'm sure we're all invited," said Kingman. "Chickie loved pets. She would have wanted us to be there."

"Are you going?" Dooley asked Kingman.

"You bet. Wouldn't miss it for the world." He abruptly turned away. Two exceedingly attractive felines had entered the store, and Kingman wouldn't be Kingman if he wasn't keen on welcoming them personally, wishing them a wonderful shopping experience.

And as Dooley and I walked out of the store, I said, "Maybe we should go to the wake. Pay our respects."

"Maybe we should," Dooley agreed. "And maybe Gran can sing her song again. As a sign of respect."

"I doubt whether that'll happen."

"But why? She's a very good singer."

"No, she's not. She's a terrible singer."

"But Charlie likes her, and Laron Weskit. And they are the experts."

"They like her because of the novelty factor. Once that wears off, they'd have dumped her like yesterday's trash. It's like those dancing poodles you see on YouTube," I explained when he gave me a look of confusion. "We all love to watch poodles dance, but people tire of them very quickly, and then they see a grinning turtle and they all flock to the turtle, giving it likes and follows, until the novelty wears off, and so on and so forth."

"You mean Gran is like a dancing poodle?"

"Or an elephant who can play the clarinet. Simply a novelty."

"Poor Gran. I don't think she knows she's like an elephant who plays the clarinet."

"I think deep down she does know."

"How about Tex? Is he a novelty?"

"No, Tex is a regular musician."

"Well, it doesn't matter. Gran makes people laugh and makes them have a good time, and that's all that matters, isn't it?"

He was right. As long as people were entertained, it didn't matter if you were a talented musician or a novelty act. And Gran certainly had a high capacity for providing entertainment.

*U*ncle Alec had asked Chase to visit Chickie's family and give them an update, and Chase had asked Odelia to tag along. Her presence, he felt, would smooth things over with the family after they'd already caught the wrong guy when they arrested Olaf the Stalker. Chickie's mother had expressed disappointment with the way the investigation was progressing, and Chase felt Odelia had established a rapport with Yuki and Nickie.

"I'm not sure it's such a good idea to bring Max and Dooley along, though," said Chase as he drove them up to the house. "Last time Max got stuck inside the coroner's office and you had to go and bail him out."

"He won't do it again," said Odelia. Max had taken such a fright that he wouldn't climb a fence or an ambulance for a long time. "Isn't that right, Max?"

"Absolutely," said Max. "No stunts from me this time. I promise."

"Or me," said Dooley.

"So why are we going back to the house, exactly?" asked Max.

"To give the family an update on the investigation," said Odelia. "Especially now with Jamie's arrest."

"Are you going to tell them I caught Jamie?" asked Dooley.

"Um… I think we better not mention that. Most people think it's a little strange when cats solve murders and talk to their humans."

"I guess you're right," said Dooley, sounding disappointed. Now that he had solved a crime he obviously felt the whole world should be informed.

"I'll tell them you helped, though. How about that?"

"You will? Oh, I would love that," said Dooley, and Odelia laughed.

"He wants to take the credit for Jamie's arrest," Odelia explained for Chase's sake.

"Can't blame him. He did a great job," said Chase. "So where are the other two?"

"I couldn't find them. Max says Harriet walked off on a huff. She wants to sing the solos in cat choir and Shanille told her it's not fair for one cat always to sing the solos and now she's upset."

"Oh, God. Cat drama. You gotta love it."

Odelia had decided to bring Max and Dooley along because she found it very hard to see Jamie as Chickie's killer. There was something they were missing, and in her experience it was always best to return to the scene of the crime and start afresh.

Chase parked the car across the road and they walked up to the gate. She recognized Tyson's voice chiming through the intercom and moments later they were buzzed in.

Yuki was waiting on the doorstep, looking nervous. "So what's the news?" she asked. "I heard you arrested Jamie? Is it true? Did she kill my daughter?"

"Let's go inside," Chase suggested.

They headed in while Max and Dooley stayed outside.

They followed Yuki into the living room and took their seats on a white leather sofa.

"So Jamie Borowiak was arrested this morning," Chase began. "And we think there's a good chance she's the person who killed your daughter."

Nickie had joined them and now sat, legs tucked underneath her, listening intently.

"Jamie? Are you sure?" she asked.

"Yes," said Odelia. "We're sure."

"You were also sure when you arrested that stalker," Yuki pointed out.

"He's been released. And he's no longer a suspect."

"Because now you have Jamie. But what makes you so sure she's the one? Did she confess?"

"No, she hasn't confessed yet," said Chase.

Odelia told them about the letter, and Yuki nodded seriously. "Pretty damning evidence," she said. "But not conclusive, wouldn't you say?"

"My uncle is interrogating her now," said Odelia. "He had to wait until her lawyer arrived. I'm sure he'll get her to confess to what she's done." She wasn't entirely sure that was the case, but she could hardly share her own doubts with the victim's family.

"I hope so," said Yuki. "Otherwise you'll have to let her go and then you still have nothing."

"As I said, we're fairly sure we have the right person in custody this time," said Chase.

"But why?" asked Yuki, wringing her hands. "Why would she do such a thing? They were BFFs. They've known each other for years. They started in the business together."

"Yeah, they were more like sisters than friends," said Nickie, frowning.

"Revenge, most likely," said Odelia.

"A fight over the boyfriend," Chase added.

"All this over that silly Charlie?" asked Yuki. She shook her head, and buried her face in her hands. "Such a shame. Such a terrible, terrible shame."

"Are you coming to the wake?" asked Nickie, changing the subject and rubbing her mother on the back.

"Yes, if that's all right with you," said Chase.

"Of course. And Chief Lip, too."

"Chickie's… body was released yesterday," said Yuki. "And the funeral director assures us he'll give her the most wonderful wake. I wanted to bury her in LA but…" Her voice broke, and Nickie took her hand in hers.

"I told Mom to bury Chickie here," said Nickie. "She loved it so much out here, so…"

"They want me to select a dress for Chickie," said Yuki. "And jewelry. But I can't find her favorite earrings. The ones her grandmother gave her."

"I'm sure they'll turn up, Mom. I'll go through her stuff again."

Her mom nodded tearfully. "Oh, why did this have to happen to us? We were so happy together."

"If you want I can help you look for the earrings," Odelia suggested, touched by Yuki's sorrow.

"That's all right," said Nickie. "I'm sure they're in her room somewhere."

"No, let her help," said Yuki. "She's a detective. This is what she does: detect."

"What do they look like?" asked Odelia.

"Um… I'll show you a picture," said Yuki. She took out her smartphone and called up a picture of Chickie wearing a pair of delicate crescent-moon golden earrings.

Yuki smiled as she studied the picture. "They belonged to my mother. Chickie was crazy about them. Wore them all the time."

"I'll have a look around while you discuss the case," Odelia said.

"Second room on the right," said Yuki. "Right next to mine."

As Odelia took the stairs two at a time, her heart hurt for Yuki. The poor woman was so distraught and grieving it was hard to bear.

She arrived upstairs and opened the door to Chickie's room. It wasn't a room, though, but more a suite of rooms. There was a living space, a bedroom, a dressing room, a yoga and meditation area and of course a large bathroom. And as she started going through Chickie's things, she suddenly felt a sense of impropriety. This wasn't really her prerogative, going through a dead person's personal items. Chickie had a lot of gorgeous things, though, all kept in a large jewelry box. And as she searched through the many rings and bracelets and earrings, she found no trace of the missing ones.

The door opened and Nickie walked in. "And? Found them?"

"No," said Odelia. "Your sister had a lot of beautiful things, though."

"Yes, she did." Nickie walked into the dressing room and called for Odelia to follow her. Nickie flicked on the light and Odelia's jaw dropped at the sight of the gorgeous collection of clothes. There were so many. Beautiful dresses, rows and rows of shoes, an entire section dedicated to underwear and lingerie...

"There's more over here," said Nickie, gesturing to a vanity. "My sister loved shopping," she explained as she took a seat on a low overstuffed sofa bench. "She could spend hours in here, and always complained she had nothing to wear." She produced a wan smile as Odelia checked the drawers in the vanity desk. There were several more boxes of jewelry there, but no crescent-moon-shaped golden earrings.

"It's hell," said Nickie somberly. "When we were little we used to fight like cats and dogs. She was born five minutes before me, and she never let me forget it. I was her little sister and so she got to boss me around. I never let her, though, hence the fights. But as we got past our teens we stopped fighting and became best friends instead. She relied on me a lot, and not just with her career. Life stuff, too. And boyfriend stuff, of course."

"So you know all about the whole Charlie Dieber thing."

"My sister and Charlie met when they were both sixteen. Boy and girl affair. It didn't last, of course. They were both too young and immature. By the time they broke up they practically hated each other. They got back together again, only to break up again. And then get back together again, etcetera etcetera."

"And then Charlie met Jamie."

"Actually the three of them had known each other for years. Jamie was Chickie's best friend, but I think secretly she'd always had feelings for Charlie. But being Chickie's friend she never acted on those feelings. Only when Chickie and Charlie broke up did she make a move. Chickie was very upset—which is probably when she wrote that letter."

"She didn't want to be with Charlie but still wasn't entirely over him either."

"Exactly."

Odelia sat back. "I'm sorry but I can't find those earrings, Nickie."

"Maybe she lost them. My sister was notoriously careless with her things."

"Or someone could have stolen them," Odelia suggested. "They look valuable."

"It's mostly the emotional value. Because they were Gram's." She got up. "Don't worry, they'll turn up sooner or later. But maybe not in time for the wake."

As they walked out of the dressing room, Nickie switched off the lights and gave Odelia a sad smile. "I miss her, you know. As if a part of me is gone now."

"I'm sorry," said Odelia, placing a consoling hand on Nickie's arm.

And then the young woman broke down in tears, possibly for the first time since her sister died. "It's only starting to dawn on me now," she said. "Chickie's gone. She's really gone and I'll never get to see her again."

They walked along the corridor when Odelia thought she caught a glimpse of Max and Dooley. Good. Hopefully they'd find a fresh clue. Yuki and Nickie deserved to get some closure, and the only way to accomplish that was by finding the real killer.

*W*e decided to forgo another meeting with the peacock and to go in search of Boyce Catt instead. It had occurred to me we'd never offered him our condolences and now seemed as good a time for that as any.

We found him in the garden, seated on one of those rustic cast-iron benches, contemplating his fate, and looking very philosophical.

"Hey there, little doggie," said Dooley, and for once the dog had no retort ready about giving Dooley two nips in his buttocks, or maybe even as much as four.

"Hey, cats," he said, sounding as dejected as he appeared.

"We never told you how sorry we are about the death of your human," I said.

"Yes, and we'd also like to tell you that we discovered who did it," Dooley added.

I could see how eager Dooley was to tell the story of the letter, so I added, "Actually Dooley here discovered the missing clue. He discovered the letter that proves that Jamie murdered your human."

"Huh," he said. "Is that a fact?" He didn't sound appropriately impressed.

"Didn't you hear what I just said? They arrested Jamie, the woman who murdered your human."

"That's great," he said, and sighed deeply. "I've been adopted by Nickie, you know."

"Nickie? But I thought you belonged to the whole family?"

"No, I was Chickie's, and now that she's gone, Nickie has decided to adopt me. She's been adopting a lot of Chickie's stuff lately. Her clothes, her car... me."

"Well, that's very nice of her, isn't it? After all, someone needs to take care of you, so why not Nickie?"

"Don't you like Nickie?" asked Dooley. "Isn't she nice?"

"Oh, she's nice enough, I guess, but not as nice as Chickie. Chickie was special, and we shared a very special bond. And now Nickie seems eager to replicate that bond but it can't be done. I can't simply transfer my affections to a new human at the drop of a hat. It takes time. I have to mourn Chickie and then, maybe, I'll be ready to let a new human into my heart."

I understood where he was coming from. If anything would ever happen to Odelia, I'd have a hard time transferring my affections, too. It probably couldn't even be done.

"At least you can stay in the same home, with the same family," I said. "Imagine having to move into a completely different home with a different family that you don't know. "

"Yeah, I guess there's that," he admitted. "Though they're going to sell the house and move west again. Yuki never liked it out here. Too chilly. And not enough sun. She prefers California, and that's where we're going after the funeral."

"So you're all moving away?"

"Yeah, the whole circus is heading west."

"And how do you feel about that?"

He shrugged. "It's okay. Maybe even for the best. After all, with Chickie gone the house just doesn't feel the same. And being in these familiar places I'm constantly reminded of her, you know. So maybe it's better to move someplace new, where everything won't remind me so much of her."

We decided to leave Boyce Catt to pine for Chickie in peace.

"So it's true that dogs feel their human's loss more intensely than cats," I said.

"He does seem to miss Chickie a lot," said Dooley.

"Poor doggie."

"Yeah, poor little doggie."

Look, I know I've said in the past that I don't like dogs all that much, but there are always exceptions to the rule, and clearly here was one of those exceptions. Boyce Catt was nice. In fact it wasn't too much to say he was almost like a cat. An honorary cat.

We wandered around a little aimlessly, and decided to take a look inside. Maybe Boyce Catt had a nice bowl of food he hadn't touched. So we walked in through the kitchen door and went in search of Boyce Catt's bowl. The kitchen didn't yield any snacks or nibbles, though, and then Dooley had a bright idea—he was on fire today.

"Remember how Boyce Catt said he lives with Nickie now?"

"Uh-huh."

"So maybe his food is in her room!"

"Great thinking, Dooley," I said, and so we padded up the stairs.

I could hear Odelia's voice coming from one of the rooms. She was talking to Chickie's sister. But Dooley and I decided to follow our noses this time, and soon we had struck gold. Prime kibble, not fifty feet away. We quickly found ourselves in a nice set of rooms, and to our elation one of the rooms had been set up as a playroom for Boyce Catt.

There were several bowls all brimming with tasty bits, and immediately we started salivating.

"Looks like Boyce Catt decided to stop eating," said Dooley.

"Looks like," I agreed, as all of the bowls were untouched.

"A loss like that will do that to a pet."

"Yes, it absolutely will."

We were silent for a beat, then shared a look. "Terrible waste of good food," said Dooley.

"Yeah, terrible waste," I echoed.

And so we tucked in. What? We're environmentally conscious cats. We don't like to see perfectly good food go to waste just because its recipient is too sad to eat it.

After we'd eaten our fill—and left plenty for Boyce Catt, I might add—we checked the rest of Nickie's apartment.

"Always nice to see how the other half lives," I told Dooley, and he agreed wholeheartedly.

There was a nice, big bedroom, an adjoining bathroom, a salon where Nickie could watch television curled up on her couch, and of course a large dressing room, with rows and rows of clothes. There was even one of those nice vanities with a dresser attached to it and Dooley had quickly jumped on top, presumably to check his look in the mirror.

Odelia had promised him a picture in her newspaper, as the cat who'd discovered the letter, and he was eager to look his absolute best for what he presumed was a photoshoot with a professional photographer. I could have told him Odelia would probably pick one of the pictures she already had of him, but had decided not to burst his bubble.

I jumped up onto the vanity, too. I glanced around, but there wasn't all that much to see. A box of jewelry, an extensive selection of nail polish and lipstick, sets of eyelashes. And as I jumped down again, I accidentally jumped into a drawer instead, and found myself knee-deep in more jewelry. With an eyeroll I jumped down, Dooley following suit.

"Let's call it a day," I said. "We ate, we sniffed around— time to get out of here."

"Do you think I need a haircut, Max?" asked Dooley as we plodded down the stairs.

"A haircut? Why? You look fine, Dooley."

"For my picture. It's not every day that I have my picture taken for the newspaper."

"We're not show cats, Dooley. We don't dress up so we can look good for the camera."

"Maybe a ribbon? A nice pink ribbon? Or a collar with flowers on it?"

"You look fine," Dooley," I said decidedly. "You don't need ribbons. Just be yourself."

"All right," he said dubiously.

We arrived at the front door just as Odelia and Chase did, and if Yuki and Nickie thought it strange to see two cats traipsing about their home, they didn't mention it.

As we were driving back to town, Odelia mentioned how she'd helped Nickie look for Chickie's crescent-moon earrings but hadn't had any luck. And that's when a memory stirred. Something important. Only it didn't immediately come to me, and then when Dooley started talking about pink ribbons and collars with flowers on them again, and asking Odelia if she thought he needed a haircut, the thought went out of my head.

*T*he wake was a peculiar affair. I don't think pets were necessarily welcome there, but Odelia didn't care what the funeral home director said. She wanted us present and keeping our eyes peeled. Why, I didn't know, as the case was now probably closed.

Harriet and Brutus were there, and me and Dooley, of course, and so was Boyce Catt. The only pet the Hays hadn't brought was Mark the Peacock. Very sensibly they'd decided to leave him at home, otherwise the wake would have turned into a real zoo.

Laron and his wife were there, and Charlie, of course, though they weren't speaking to the Pooles, clearly blaming them for Jamie's arrest. I didn't think this was fair, to be honest. After all, Jamie only had herself to blame. She shouldn't have murdered her former best friend.

The pets had all been relegated to a space near the front of the room, and so we sat on the floor, next to Boyce Catt, who couldn't stop howling, unfortunately, and after a while was discreetly led away by a well-dressed man who worked for the funeral home.

The wake was one endless line of people wanting to say goodbye to Chickie, who was a very popular person. Several people had flown in especially for the wake and tomorrow's funeral. Finally, Harriet and Brutus decided to leave, due to a bladder emergency—the wake did drag on a little too long for my taste—and then it was only me and Dooley. The room had emptied out at this point, with most people talking softly in the next room, reminiscing and sharing stories of Chickie.

A lone figure walked up to the coffin, which had been placed on a small dais, surrounded by little white flowers. The figure, who turned out to be Nickie, now stood gazing down at the dead pop singer's body.

"Odd, isn't it, Max?" said Dooley.

"What is, Dooley?" I said, starting to feel a pressing concern in the region of my bladder, too.

"She doesn't look dead. She looks as if she's about to wake up any moment now and burst into song and dance."

He was right. The mortician had done a great job and Chickie looked fresh as a daisy. As if she wasn't dead but merely taking a light nap, soon to rise, happy and refreshed.

"I'm so sorry," suddenly spoke Nickie, after darting a quick glance around her. "But you left me no choice, Chickie! All those years treating me like I was your servant and not your little sister. Anyone could see it wouldn't end well. And now they've gone and arrested that stupid Jamie. Serves her well. I never liked her anyway, and neither did you, did you, Chickie? Anyway, I'm sure you'll learn to forgive me, and I have to admit I've felt nothing but relief since you've been gone. I thought I'd feel intense grief but so far, nothing. Only relief. Relief finally to be free again. Free to be my own person, and not just Chickie's sister. Your personal slave. And I promise you we'll take care of your legacy, big sister. We'll make sure you're not forgotten, and money from all that music you made keeps rolling in. I'll spend it all in your honor. Now rest peacefully, my sweet." She reached out a hand and touched her sister's face, then hurriedly tripped off again.

Both Dooley and I just sat there, stunned.

"Do you realize what just happened, Dooley?" I said finally.

"I think Uncle Alec arrested the wrong person, Max," he said.

"I think so, too."

And then I realized something else. "Dooley, I totally forgot, but those missing crescent-moon earrings Odelia mentioned? I think I've seen them in Nickie's dressing room. She must have taken them from her sister and kept them for herself."

"We have to tell Odelia."

"Yes, we do."

"She won't be happy."

"Why not? We just caught Chickie's killer."

"Yeah, but after we caught the wrong killer first."

I patted his shoulder consolingly. "It can happen to anyone, Dooley. Uncle Alec arrested the wrong killer first, when he decided that stalker guy did it."

But Dooley looked genuinely upset. "I really thought I'd caught the right one, Max."

"I know, Dooley. But at least now you caught the right one."

"There is that," he admitted.

Moments later, Odelia returned, looking for us.

"Hey, you guys," she said. "Time to go home."

She must have sensed something was wrong, for she suddenly turned serious.

"What's the matter?"

And when we told her about Nickie's little goodbye

speech to her sister, her face turned even more grave than before.

"Well, I'll be damned," she said.

ickie Hay was humming one of her sister's hits as she sat in front of her vanity and admired her new hairstyle. Her hairstylist had fashioned it for the wake and she loved it. It had cost a pretty penny but that was fine. She was rolling in money now, with no one to tell her not to spend it. Tomorrow at the funeral she was going to give a tearful farewell to her big sister, and then it was off to California where a new life awaited.

She opened the dresser drawer and picked out her gram's earrings, then after a moment's hesitation put them in. Admiring her look in the mirror, she smiled.

"They look much better on me than on you, big sis," she murmured.

Suddenly she thought she heard a noise behind her. She looked up and was startled to find that Mom had entered the room, and brought that annoying reporter with her.

Quickly she removed the earrings and returned them to the drawer.

"It's no use, Nickie," said her mother. "I know you took your sister's earrings. There's no point denying."

"Hi, Odelia," she said, ignoring her mother's comment. "To what do we owe the pleasure? Again?" she added with a touch of pique. When were the police finally going to leave them in peace?

"I know what you did, Nickie," said Odelia. "I know you killed your sister. Because you felt oppressed by her, and because without her you would finally be able to shine."

Nickie stared at the woman. How did she... "You're kidding, right? Only this morning you told us you caught the killer. That Jamie was the one that did it."

"Oh, stop with the charade," said Mom. "The police had the funeral home bugged. They were hoping the real killer would expose themselves, and you did."

Nickie's heart skipped a beat and she suddenly felt hot and cold at the same time. She couldn't breathe. "The police did what?" she asked in a strangled voice. Her hand had stolen out and was casually opening one of the dresser drawers.

"We heard what you said, Nickie. Your confession. Word for word. So you see? There's no point denying."

"Did you come alone?" Nickie asked, trying to see beyond Odelia and her mom.

"The police are right outside," said Mom. "They wanted to give us a moment before they arrested you. Why, Nickie? Why did you do it?"

Nickie had her hand already fastened around the pearl-inlaid grip of a small handgun. The one she'd bought as part of a matching set. She and Chickie had gotten them after they'd suffered another stalker scare. But she quickly realized she couldn't get out of this one. If what Odelia said was true, and the police were waiting outside...

She decided the jig was up and fixed her mother with a pleading look. "Don't you see, Mom? I had to get rid of her."

Mom heaved a stifled sob, as if only now realizing it was

really true. That she really had killed her one and only sibling.

"I don't understand. How could you?"

"Easy. In fact I've been wanting to do it for a long time," she said softly. "You couldn't see it, because she was always your favorite, but she had a controlling and monstrous side. She treated me as her personal slave from the moment she had her first hit. Told me what to do, what to wear, what to say. Never once did she stop to think I was a person, with my own dreams and desires. She always came first. I just couldn't take it anymore."

"So why didn't you leave? Why didn't you tell her you didn't want to be her personal assistant anymore and left?"

Nickie laughed. "Did you ever try to say no to Chickie, Mom? You know what she was like. I told her once I was thinking about using my MBA. Maybe start my own company. She got so upset. Accused me of trying to sabotage her career. Said this was a family business and I better get in line or else. Problem was, because I'd been living in her shadow for so long I wasn't even sure what exactly I wanted to do with my life. What person I was without her. She suffocated me, Mom," she said, a quiver in her voice.

"But... you killed your sister, honey. You... *murdered* her."

"I know. It was the only way to get rid of her. The only way to be free. And you know what? It feels good. For the first time in a long while I'm starting to feel like myself again."

"You do realize you're going to jail, don't you, Nickie?" asked Odelia.

"Even in jail I'll be better off than being Chickie's slave," she said, and meant it.

There was a squeaky sound, and Odelia said, "Did you get all that, Chase?"

"Loud and clear," a staticky voice sounded through the room. "We're coming in."

Nickie relaxed her hand and dropped the gun back in its hiding place, then closed the drawer. She wasn't going to get out of there, gun blazing. That was so not her style.

"Why did you steal your sister's earrings?" asked Mom. "That, I don't understand."

Her expression hardened. "They were never Chickie's, Mom. Gram gave them to both of us, so we could share them. But of course Chickie took them for herself, even though she knew how much they meant to me. So I took them back. She wore them long enough. Now it's my turn."

"They won't let you wear them in prison, honey," said Mom, looking heartbroken.

"I'll wear them when I get out."

"Oh, honey," said Mom and shook her head, then burst into tears.

"Cheer up, Mom," she said. "You lost one daughter, but you gained another." She smiled. "And I'm finally happy. Isn't that what you always wanted?"

EPILOGUE

$\mathcal{T}$he Poole family was gathered in Marge and Tex's backyard, the humans enjoying Tex's talents at the grill, and the cats going over the events of the past week. Things had suddenly turned extremely eventful. With the death of Chickie Hay and the arrest of her sister, the world media had suddenly descended upon Hampton Cove en masse.

Nickie had asked to be allowed to attend her sister's funeral, and Uncle Alec had finally agreed, which had created quite a ruckus. The Mayor hadn't been happy. He also hadn't been happy with the ruse about the funeral home being bugged, which it hadn't. It was still better than the truth: that two cats had overheard Nickie's confession. And the ruse had worked: Nickie had made a full confession, this time in court in front of the judge.

Jamie had been released from prison, with apologies from Uncle Alec on behalf of the entire police department, and she and Charlie had immediately left town, along with Laron and Shannon Weskit. They probably didn't want to risk being arrested again. They'd threatened to sue the police department but I don't think they'd go through with it. Uncle Alec's suspicions had been well founded, and the man wasn't infallible. Dooley had felt bad about the whole thing for a while, but I'd told him we all make mistakes, and in the end we did solve the murder. When at first you don't succeed and all that, right?

"They turned me down!" said Gran. "Can you believe it? I invited Laron and his wife over for dinner and they turned me down flat! Didn't even apologize or nothing. Skipped town like a couple of crooks."

"Celebrities don't like to spend time in jail," said Uncle Alec. "It makes them look bad in the eyes of their fanbase."

"Except if you're a gangster rapper," said Tex, expertly flipping a burger patty and sending it sailing straight into the bushes.

"Tex is right," said Chase as he walked up to the grill and graciously took the tongs from Tex. "Gangster rappers want to be arrested. It's good for their street cred."

Tex, who'd picked up the patty and was now checking it for ants and dirt, said, "We've actually been thinking about incorporating a rap routine into our show. Rap is all the rage now, so we might as well take advantage and appeal to a younger demographic."

Gran tolled her eyes. Ever since her own career had tanked, she didn't want to hear about how well The Singing Doctors were doing. Tex was still only playing local gigs, but then he'd never had any ambitions of doing anything else. He enjoyed hanging out with his two friends and had fun making music. Stardom was the last thing on their minds.

"I'm just glad you didn't get shot, honey," said Marge, who'd placed a large bowl of potato salad on the table. "When I heard that Nickie had a gun in her dresser drawer…"

"She would never have used that gun," said Odelia.

"I'm not so sure about that," said Uncle Alec, who'd opened a bottle of beer and now took a swig. "She told us she actually thought about fleeing the scene when you walked in on her, but when she realized police were there, she dropped the idea. Said dying in a hail of bullets didn't appeal to her all that much. So you were lucky, Odelia. Very lucky."

Odelia gulped a little at that, and so did the four of us.

"So Odelia was in actual danger, Max?" asked Dooley.

"Looks like it," I said.

"We should have been there," said Harriet, tsk-tsking freely. "Why didn't she take us along for this big confrontation? We could have saved her if things turned nasty."

"And how would you have done that?" I asked. "If someone pulls a gun on you, how would you stop them?"

"Easy. I would jump on top of them and dig my claws and teeth in," said Harriet.

"I would throw myself in front of the bullet," said Brutus, puffing out his chest. "Anything to save my human from harm."

"Would you throw yourself in front of a bullet to save Odelia, Max?" asked Dooley.

"I don't know, Dooley," I said. "It's one of those things you don't know until they happen to you."

"Nonsense," said Brutus. "I know for a fact I would do it, no doubt about it."

"And yet I don't think you would, Brutus," I said. "When the moment arrives, I think it's a rare cat that would happily take a bullet for their human."

"Dogs would do it," said Dooley. "Dogs would take a bullet for their human."

We all thought about this for a moment. There was a lot of truth in what Dooley said.

Then Brutus grumbled, "Yeah, but we all know that's

because dogs are too dumb to realize the consequences of their actions. Act first, think later is the dog's way."

"True," Harriet said. "Dogs probably think the bullet is a fly they need to catch."

We all laughed at this. Well, it's true, isn't it? The reason dogs jump at the chance to catch bullets for their humans is simply because they don't realize bullets are dangerous things that can do actual damage.

Thus reassured that dogs are, in fact, the inferior species, we all greeted Odelia with cheers when she brought us some fresh burger patties, straight from Tex's—now Chase's—grill. And as we all tucked in, Dooley said, "I still feel sorry I put Jamie in jail."

"Oh, Dooley!" Harriet cried. "Not again with the whole Jamie thing."

"But it was my fault she was arrested, and I can't help feeling bad about it."

"I think that time spent in jail was probably the best thing that ever happened to Jamie," I said, patting my friend on the back. "Besides, I thought that letter was the real deal, too, remember? So this is my fault, too."

He gave me a hopeful look. "You really think so, Max?"

"Of course. I told you to go and give that letter to Gran."

"No, about spending time in jail being good for Jamie."

"Of course. A good artist needs to suffer. Because of you, Jamie is a better artist now."

"Not sure she feels the same way," Brutus muttered.

"And I'm sure she does," said Harriet, giving me a wink.

Dooley had perked up considerably at this, and was now eating his burger with relish. "You know?" he said finally, munching happily, "maybe we should tell Uncle Alec that Gran committed murder. That way she'll become a better artist, too. She'll like that."

"Um…" I said, alarmed.

"And how about Tex! He sure could use the encouragement. In fact why don't we tell the Chief *all* of the singing doctors are nasty, vicious killers? They'll be so, so grateful!"

"Um, Dooley, I don't think that's such a good idea," I said.

"Why? Gran wants to be a star, and this might put her over the top. And Tex, too."

"Gran and Tex want to be *local* stars, not international ones like Jamie. So they don't need that big push that Jamie received when she was arrested."

He thought about this for a moment, champing quietly. Then he nodded. "I think I get it, Max. Murder is too big a crime for Gran and Tex. What they want is a small crime. Just a little one. So how about a nice burglary? Or shoplifting? Or no, wait, I've got it!" He fixed me with a beaming smile. "Pickpocketing! We could say they picked our pockets!"

Harriet suppressed a chuckle, and so did Brutus. They gave me a look that said, 'Try and wriggle your way out of this one, Max.' And I had to confess I was starting to regret using the prison ruse to cheer my friend up.

"Cats don't have pockets to pick, Dooley," said Harriet. "So that wouldn't work."

Once more, Dooley was plunged in thought, then finally his face cleared. "We'll say Gran picked Tex's pockets and Tex picked Gran's pockets! Kill two stones with one bird!"

"The other way around, Dooley," I said.

"Fine. We'll say Tex picked Gran's pockets and Gran picked Tex's pockets."

Well, it was a solution of a sort, and an elegant one, too. I didn't have the heart to tell Dooley it was also unrealistic. So I pointed behind him. "Oh, my God, look at the size of that butterfly!"

"What, where?!" Dooley cried, swiveling his head like a whirligig.

"Darn it, you just missed it."

And as Dooley scanned the horizon for the elusive giant butterfly, I shared a smile with Brutus and Harriet. Through long association with Dooley I've learned the best way to solve any tricky issue with my dear friend: the art of distraction. Works every time.

By the time Dooley had come to terms with the fact that he had missed this rare sighting, he'd forgotten all about his scheme to propel Gran and Tex to stardom.

And a good thing, too.

As the afternoon wore on and turned to dusk, the scent of meat sizzling on the grill and the soft chattering of our humans caused my eyes to gradually drift closed, and soon I was dozing peacefully. I would have told you I dreamt of accolades being showered on us for our detective work, of prizes being awarded by the town's notables, or even the keys of the city being granted to the four of us. But if I'm absolutely honest with you—and when am I ever not?—I'd have to confess that all I dreamt about was a nice bowl of kibble, a soft pillow to stretch out on, my friends nearby, and my human gently stroking my fur.

Cats. So easy to please. And if anyone tells you differently, he's probably a dog.

I awoke from my peaceful slumber when Dooley gave me a gentle prod in the ribs.

"What is it, Dooley?" I said, and when I opened my eyes found him staring at me.

"Max? You still haven't told me."

"Told you what, Dooley?"

"So… who is Beyoncé?"

EXCERPT FROM THE WHISKERED
SPY

1. The Brookridge Park Horror

I was sitting in an elm tree looking down at the world below, minding my own business, when the stirring events I'm about to relate took place. As it happens, it was my favorite tree to sit and watch the world go by while licking any part of my anatomy that needed licking. Not that I'm a philosopher, per se. But I'm a cat and, closely following Chapter 3, Paragraph 6, Section 8 of the Cat Guild Book of Regulations, sitting in trees is a task highly recommended to fill at least one time slot a day, an average time slot equaling more or less 7 human hours. And it was as the last minutes of my tree-sitting time for the day were ticking away, that I became aware of strange happenings down on the ground below.

The perch I had chosen for my tree time was located in the middle of the Brookridge park, which has, among its many other points of interest, a very large population of birds that like to occupy its various trees—closely following the rules of *their* particular guild. And as everyone knows, chasing birds is clearly outlined in Chapter 1 of the Cat Guild rulebook as one of the mainstays of an adult cat's life. But apart from cats, trees and birds, another life form habitually infests the Brookridge park: humans. And it were two members of this odd species who were now hobnobbing under my tree's foliage.

Clearly laboring under the misapprehension that they were alone, they were speaking in the hushed tones of the professional hobnobber. I pricked up my ears and studied the duo intently. One was a female human, oddly enough dressed up in white, as if preparing to attend a wedding, the other a male. And for a moment I had labeled their actions as part of the mating ritual humans like to observe: first they spend the longest time talking, then some form of physical contact follows, and finally they start locking lips, something I've never been able to endure with fortitude.

And I was about to hop to the next tree and save myself the sickening spectacle, when words reached my ears that perked me up considerably.

"I think he's on to us," said the female.

"Are you sure?" said the male.

No reply followed, but from the next sentence spoken by the male, it was obvious the woman had given him some form of nonverbal confirmation.

"That's too bad," he said. "That means we'll have to take him out."

I can tell you right now that my tail shivered from stem to stern at these words. 'Take him out'. That could only mean... Here, through some form of divine intervention, I had stumbled upon a secret meeting between two spies! I knew of course that Brookridge is a veritable nest of spies and its local park their favorite hangout, but it was the first time I'd ever encountered two real-life spies in the flesh. And under my favorite tree no less! Talk about ringside seats.

The woman gasped. "Take him out!" she said. It was obvious to me that she didn't agree with her fellow spy's assessment of the situation. "Are you nuts?"

"Nuts about you," whispered the man. "And I'll be damned if I'm going to let that little weasel get in the way of our future happiness. Either he goes, or I go."

"No! Jack!" cried the woman. "Don't go!"

At these words, my tail stopped shivering and my ears flopped. This was not the talk of two spies planning to take out some unfortunate competitor, but of two lovers, plotting to do away with a husband or wife or possibly both. I heaved a deep sigh to signify the premature dashing of all my hopes and dreams and languidly trotted to the edge of the branch I'd been sitting on to prepare for my departure from the lurid scene. It no longer held any interest for me.

Unfortunately, just in that moment, another cat arrived on the scene and engaged me in conversation. It was Dana, the highly strung Siamese belonging to one of the neighbors.

"Hello, Tom," she said in her customary sultry voice. "What are you doing out so late? Don't you have to be home with daddy around this time of night?"

"Hi there, Dana," I said in my most casual way. "Where did you spring from all of a sudden?"

"Oh, I was just hopping around here and there, checking out the neighborhood, when I happened to run into Stevie. You know Stevie, don't you? Father Sam's Ragamuffin?"

Yes, I knew Stevie. The mongrel ate a mouse I'd marked for my own one night when I wasn't watching. "Shh," I said, for I noticed Dana's jabbering had interrupted the easy flow of conversation coming from the couple downstairs.

"Shh, yourself," said Dana, amused. "No one shushes me, Tom. You know that. As I was saying, I ran into Stevie and noticed he'd done something different with his whiskers. They seemed, I don't know, longer or something. So I said,

'Stevie. I like what you've done with your whiskers. What's your secret?' And Stevie said, 'Extensions. It's the new craze.' And I said—"

"Will you please be quiet!" I hissed. For my sensitive ears had picked up something else now. The woman had begun softly sobbing and the man was now whispering something consoling into her ear and patting her gently on the back. It wasn't this patting on the back that worried me, though, but the long and shiny butcher's knife he was pulling out of his pocket with his free hand and carefully poising behind the woman's back.

"Well, I never," said Dana, shocked at being spoken to like that by a mere tabby.

But then I directed her attention to the two people down below, and when she saw the moonlight glitter on the knife, she let rip a cry so piercing, it stayed the hand of the man just on the verge of plunging the knife into the woman's back. Both the man and the woman looked up to see what all the ruckus was about.

"He's got a knife!" trilled Dana.

I rolled my eyes at this piece of old news. "I can see that," I said. "And it looks like he's not afraid to use it."

"But then, he's a murderer!" cried Dana.

"Yah," I said. "Obviously."

"We have to stop him. Oh, Tom, do something!"

Now, humans habitually call for help on these occasions. Well, you're a human. You know the drill. You yell, 'Police! Help!', at the top of your lungs and more often than not someone will show up. Unfortunately, we cats can yell all we want but no police or help will show up. What we can do is cry our little hearts out, though, and if we're lucky, one of those fellows with a hard hat and a red coat will come running and save us from the tree. Firemen, I think humans call them. Exceedingly fine fellows I've always thought, and I'm on a first-name basis with most of Brookridge's finest.

"Let's pretend we're stuck in this tree and perhaps a fireman will show up," I said therefore.

"But why?" said Dana, frowning confusedly. "We're not stuck in this tree."

"I know we're not stuck in this tree, but that woman down there is going to get it in the neck if we don't do something quick!"

Her eyes lit up with the dim light of intelligence. "Oh, I see. We yell for help and when one of those nice red men show up, the killer will think twice about doing whatever he—"

She didn't finish her sentence for she had happened to glance down and I saw every thew and sinew in her slender body stiffen with apprehension. Following her gaze I started. The woman was now lying facedown on the grass, the man standing over her with the knife still in his hand. He was cleaning it methodically with a large handkerchief.

2. Murder in the Park

"He did it!" cried Dana. "He murdered that poor, poor woman!"

I wanted to point out that for all we knew the woman had simply decided to take a nap, the man preparing to butter a piece of toast for when she woke up, but it was obvious Dana was right for a change: a murder had taken place and we were both eyewitnesses.

"Dang," I said, as I stared my eyes out at the murder scene. It doesn't happen every day that you see a murder take place. Now, mind you, we hadn't actually seen 'it' happen, more like the before and after. But it wasn't hard to imagine what had happened in between. When you see a fellow raise a knife behind a woman's back and next thing you know the woman is lying lifeless on the ground and the man is cleaning the knife, the thing speaks for itself.

Dana, who was sobbing for dear life, suddenly turned on me with a vengeance. "It's all your fault," she cried. "If you hadn't started blabbing on and on about firemen, we could have saved that poor woman."

"Huh?" I said, too stunned to construct a decent retort.

Dana wrung her paws. "I should have simply jumped down on that awful man's back, claws extended. He wouldn't have been so eager to go sticking knives in innocent women's backs then. Or perhaps I should have jumped on his head and clawed at his nose. God knows I've done it before. Works like magic every time."

I shivered, and this time it wasn't from the sight of the gruesome scene down below, but from a slight apprehension at finding myself within striking distance of Dana's claws. I'm a big boy and I pride myself on my powers of self-defense, but when I encounter dames of Dana's obvious level of ferociousness, I respectfully bow out.

I started to do so now, but Dana stopped me with word and gesture. The gesture being a tap on my head and the word a menacing growl.

"Where do you think you're going?" she said.

"Ouch," I said, and rubbed the spot where she'd tapped me. "Home. Where else?"

"Home?" she cried, visibly appalled. "How can you talk about going home with this murder going on right under our noses. We have to…"

I gave her a wry smile. "We have to what? There's nothing we can do. The police will take care of everything."

"But, we know who did it. We can help the police."

I scoffed. "We're just cats. We can't help the police. We can't do a single thing."

"But, but…"

"I'm going home," I said, and turned to leave.

A searing pain in my left buttock made me change my mind. "On second thought…" I said, and watched as Dana licked her claws.

"We can't let murderer boy get away with this," Dana said. "Stevie would never…"

"Oh, please," I said. "Not Stevie again. That bird-brain wouldn't do a single thing."

"Oh, yes, he would," said Dana, adamant. "Stevie's got more courage in one whisker than you have in that grue-somely large body of yours."

"My body isn't gruesomely large," I said, slightly offended.

"Yes, it is," she said. "We don't call you Fat Tom around the neighborhood for nothing."

"No one calls me Fat Tom," I said, appalled at the slur.

"We do, you know," said Dana with a smirk that didn't become her.

"For your information, I'm not fat," I said as haughtily as I could. "I'm just big, that's all. Large bone structure, Zack always says." Zack Zapp is, as the vernacular goes, my owner. Though I might as well add that no one really owns me, as I'm a free spirit. Well, that is until my stomach starts making funny noises and it comes time to have a stab at the cat bowl and find out what's for lunch.

"Then Zack is as big a chump as you are," Dana said decidedly. "Now, what are you going to do about that murdering fellow downstairs?"

"Nothing," I said, after throwing a glance at the ground floor. "Because he's legged it."

Dana, after ascertaining my observation was correct, frowned thoughtfully. "And so did she."

I did a double take at these words. It doesn't often happen that dead bodies get up and take off. Looking again, I saw that she was right: both the killer and the killee, if that's the word I want, had removed themselves from the scene.

"That's odd," I remarked. "Usually on these occasions the corpse stays put."

"Unless the killer took it with him."

"As a souvenir, you mean?"

Dana sighed. "Stevie was right about you. You really are a dumb brick."

"I am not! Humans often take souvenirs. When Zack came back from England he brought a pipe and a tea pot."

"A dead body is not a tea pot, Tom."

I had to admit she had a point there. At least a tea pot serves some purpose, no matter how small, whereas a dead body is of no use to anyone.

She reflected. "The killer is obviously trying to hide the body. Would you recognize him when you saw him again?"

I said I probably could. For when the fellow had looked up I'd taken a good look at his face. Nothing to write home about, mind you. Just one of those average human faces. Fortunately for me—Dana was extending those claws of hers once more—I'd spotted one distinguishable feature about the killer's face: a pimple.

"He had a large pimple on the tip of his nose," I said triumphantly as I kept a close eye on Dana's paws. "Unless it was a fly temporarily using the man's face as a launching pad." I gave a hearty laugh at my own joke. Dana didn't laugh.

"A killer with a pimple," she said. "And a dead body that has suddenly disappeared. Right." She got up and started threading her way down the branches of the tree.

"Hey, where are you going?" I said. For, though I was feeling relieved to finally be rid of her, I was also a bit peeved at the abruptness of her departure.

"I'm going to get help," she said, without looking back.

"Help? From whom?" Perhaps it should have been 'who', but whatever it was, Dana didn't deign to reply. The night swallowed her up and before long she was gone.

I shrugged and after having given the matter some more thought—do teapots really have more use than a human corpse? After all, a human body can be used as compost, whereas a teapot merely serves as an eyesore—I trotted off myself. A midnight snack and a warm bed were awaiting me and a tall tale to tell my friends bubbled on my lips.

3. The Third Degree

I'd pretty much forgotten all about recent events, when a bark arrested my progress towards the homestead. It was Frank, the neighborhood watchdog. I know, watchdog isn't much of a way to describe any dog, but it's how we like to call him around these parts. Frank is in fact a Poodle—complete with woolly coat and docked tail—and fancies himself something of a local law enforcement officer. In other words, our very own flattie.

"Evening, Tommy," he said in his customary gravelly voice.

"Evening, Frank," I said, refusing, as usual, to address him as 'officer', something he's quite keen on.

"I just met Dana," he said, and cocked an inquisitive eye at me. I didn't take the bait and he continued. "She said she was a witness to some funny business happening in the park just now and you were also present at the scene. Care to comment?"

I sighed. So this was the help Dana had gone and found. "Yes, Frank," I said curtly, for what I wanted more than anything was to go home and have a bite to eat. Kibble and a bowl of milk awaited me. "I saw one human slash another human and then make off with the body. And no, I really don't think it is any of our business. If humans want to slay each other, fine. As long as they don't start in on any of our kind, I really don't see why we should get involved."

Frank waggled his ears. "Oh, so that's how you see it, is it?"

"That's how I see it, Frank," I said. As long as the humans keep the kibble coming, of course, but I didn't voice this thought to the self-appointed keeper of the peace.

"Well, now," he said, with a hint of reproach. "Isn't that kind of selfish?"

"No, it is not," I assured him.

"Then let me ask you this," he said. "What if that woman who'd just been brutally murdered was Zack? How would you feel about the situation then?"

I hate to admit it but the fluffy one had a point there. Apart from the fact that Zack was a man and not a woman, I probably would have felt differently if he'd been the one on the receiving end of the knife just then. "Well…" I said, trying to come up with something glib and witty.

"I thought so," Frank said with a grunt of satisfaction. "Selfish to a degree; that's the Tom I know."

"I'm not selfish," I protested, but I knew he had me licked. It's not just that Zack provides me with all the necessaries like food and shelter, I'm also quite partial to the way he tickles me under my chin and strokes my whiskers. And the way he fluffs up my pillow each time before I take a nap is also one of those things that endears him to me in ways that I find hard to describe to anyone but my closest friends. I do believe he loves me, if you catch my drift, and I have to admit to being quite fond of the big oaf as well.

"Look, that's neither here nor there. The fact of the matter is that Zack is not the one going around being stabbed in parks at night. He's too smart to ever get himself entangled with a cold-blooded murderer like that. And for one thing, the woman was cheating on her husband, so…"

Frank cocked an eye. "And that makes it all right for her to be whacked by some psycho in the local park?"

"No, that's not what I meant," I said quickly. Oh, boy, I really was sinking deeper and deeper into the quagmire. Perhaps I should just shut my big mouth and move on before I really got myself into trouble with the furry arm of the law. "What I meant was that…" To tell you the truth, I didn't really know what I meant.

"Right," said Frank. "Not only selfish to a degree, but also sexist. I see."

"Look, I understand the desire to make a character study of my person, but don't you have something better to do? Like to search for men with pimples on the tips of their noses? I'm sure Dana told you about that telling detail?"

Frank nodded, his ears flopping to and fro as he did. "She did, indeed. But I was hoping to extract some more details from you. Like what kind of clothes was he wearing? What color was his hair, his eyes, his face? Was he tall? Small? Fat? Skinny? What did he smell like?"

On and on the interrogation went. I supplied the good Poodle with all the details I could remember and finally, after what seemed like an interminable delay, I was finally released from Frank's scrutinizing gaze, and allowed to go on my merry way.

It still puzzled me a great deal why this self-appointed upholder of the law would go to all the trouble of conducting a police investigation in what clearly was a human affair, when my progress towards the kibble trough was halted once again. By then I'd reached the edge of the park and was trotting down the sidewalk, having once more managed to relegate the sordid details of the recent affair to the back of my mind.

A sudden hiss arrested my attention, and when I turned to verify its source, I found myself staring into the eyes of Brutus, my nemesis, staring back at me from the shrubbery.

ABOUT NIC

Nic Saint is the pen name for writing couple Nick and Nicole Saint. They've penned novels in the romance, cat sleuth, middle grade, suspense, comedy and cozy mystery genres. Nicole has a background in accounting and Nick in political science and before being struck by the writing bug the Saints worked odd jobs around the world (including massage therapist in Mexico, gardener in Italy, restaurant manager in India, and Berlitz teacher in Belgium).

When they're not writing they enjoy Christmas-themed Hallmark movies (whether it's Christmas or not), all manner of pastry, comic books, a daily dose of yoga (to limber up those limbs), and spoiling their big red tomcat Tommy.

www.nicsaint.com

Nora Steel

Murder Retreat

The Kellys

Murder Motel

Death in Suburbia

Emily Stone

Murder at the Art Class

Washington & Jefferson

First Shot

Alice Whitehouse

Spooky Times

Spooky Trills

Spooky End

Spooky Spells

Ghosts of London

Between a Ghost and a Spooky Place

Public Ghost Number One

Ghost Save the Queen

Box Set 1 (Books 1-3)

A Tale of Two Harrys

Ghost of Girlband Past

Ghostlier Things

Charleneland

Deadly Ride

Final Ride

Neighborhood Witch Committee

Witchy Start

Witchy Worries

Witchy Wishes

Saffron Diffley

Crime and Retribution

Vice and Verdict

Felonies and Penalties (Saffron Diffley Short 1)

The B-Team

Once Upon a Spy

Tate-à-Tate

Enemy of the Tates

Ghosts vs. Spies

The Ghost Who Came in from the Cold

Witchy Fingers

Witchy Trouble

Witchy Hexations

Witchy Possessions

Witchy Riches

Box Set 1 (Books 1-4)

The Mysteries of Bell & Whitehouse

One Spoonful of Trouble

Two Scoops of Murder

Three Shots of Disaster

Box Set 1 (Books 1-3)

A Twist of Wraith

A Touch of Ghost

A Clash of Spooks

Box Set 2 (Books 4-6)

The Stuffing of Nightmares

A Breath of Dead Air

An Act of Hodd

Box Set 3 (Books 7-9)

A Game of Dons

Standalone Novels

When in Bruges

The Whiskered Spy

ThrillFix

Homejacking

The Eighth Billionaire

The Wrong Woman

Printed in Great Britain
by Amazon